The Ghost of a Lost Love

C S Lewando

Free Offers
at the end of the novel

Chapter 1

Stephanie first went to Townsea by chance.

It was a small fishing village on the South Devon coast, where cobbled streets and ancient cob cottages led down to a tiny harbour. She needed to wash the city from her soul for a brief time; hear the sound of seagulls, breathe salt air, and remember there was life beyond the office. She wasn't worried where she might land, as long it wasn't too far to drive, and offered diving trips. Townsea had all that, and a holiday-let that wasn't out of reach, financially.

Her flat-mate, Rachel had laughed. 'Jesus, you could go to Tenerife or Majorca for less,' she said.

But Stephanie's experience of foreign holidays hadn't always been good ones. Alone under a foreign sun was still alone, and there was the problem of being seen to be available. She'd experienced the expectation of foreign youths who supposed a solitary English girl was obviously asking for it. She thought Townsea would be safer, and if she wasn't enjoying herself, she could simply drive home.

It was early in the season, before the algae bloom would muddy the crystal Atlantic waters. She'd contacted the local dive shop before her arrival, so was expected.

And there, she discovered her dive guide was an English youth with the looks and charisma of a Greek god. Tass, with his sun-bleached hair, his beautiful green eyes, and his perfect body, tanned by sun and wind.

He was younger than her by eight years; but she wouldn't be the first woman to be attracted to a younger man, nor he a man attracted to an older woman. They had a lot in common, and the age difference just wasn't a factor.

She told him, when they first met, *I don't do holiday romances*. Yet, they'd made love before the night was out. He'd been selfish in his courtship, storming her defences with insistent pressure, and when she'd given in, it had been gladly. No seduction had ever been more welcome.

In fact, being seduced so determinedly was a novel experience, one she doubted she would ever know again. He was a raw component of life itself, part of the sea, as basic as nature, and she loved every moment she spent in his company. They drank beer, surfed and snorkelled, and in the evenings, they made love.

It was magical.

The weather was unseasonably kind, the sun burning the beach with almost Mediterranean intensity.

They dived the Southey Lad together, sleek as seals in their wetsuits, enjoying the weightless freedom, watching bubbles from their regulators explode into the roof spaces. In shafts of sunlight that cut down into the depth, they watched the fish idle through the cracked metal plates, and dart over the bed of shells and stones and crabs and trailing weed. The wreck had seemed strong, then; a towering iron structure in a dislocated world, with its underwater rooms, its stairwells that could be swum down headfirst, and its vast, silent engine.

Those two magical weeks were followed by a tearful parting, and the promise of further contact.

And that was the last she heard of him.

For a few months afterwards, in the monotonous round of work and home, Stephanie wondered if Tass had been thinking of her, or even if he remembered her. As time went by, she came to the rueful conclusion that she'd had a classic holiday romance with a charming beach bum. But there was a slight chance he'd simply lost her number. She was almost certain she was chasing rainbows but had to know.

Stephanie arrived in Townsea at lunch time to find the dive shop closed for the season, but there was a gift shop open. The bell tinkled as she went in.

'Can I help you?' the woman behind the counter asked.

'Do you know where I can find Tass?'

The woman looked slightly disconcerted, then her face softened. 'Tass died, love, didn't you know?'

The almost clinical statement shocked Stephanie, but what other way could it have been said? She walked numbly down the esplanade. The vibrant, beautiful Tass was dead?

How was that even possible?

Presumably everyone who mattered knew: Tass's relatives and huge circle of friends. They would all have mourned him, not thinking of his holiday girl-friend, or wondering whether she cared.

She trawled his usual haunts in a daze, and discovered a little more from the old man who worked the fishing-boat winch.

'Tass Purdy? Sure, he drowned out on the wreck back in the summer.' He shook his head. 'Always thought he'd come to a sticky end, too cocky by far.'

'He drowned?' she whispered. 'How?'

'Diving out alone. Never could take advice, that boy.' The old man's eyes were glued to his gnarled hands which were scraping rust from a vast hook with a wire brush. He turned it over and surveyed it. 'Ay. Sad day. He should have had more care to the sea, though. Ever a harsh mistress, that one. Can't take her for granted, eh? But Tass never did want to lift a finger to do an honest day's work, not like his kin wanted.'

He was wallowing in his story, and had probably told it a thousand times to a thousand holiday-makers. But what right did that old man have to be so dismissive? Who could blame Tass for refusing to go trawling, to learn a dying trade that was dangerous and dirty? Who could blame him for making the most of his youth, for enjoying the call of the sea? He'd been too vital and aware of a future to earn callouses hauling nets and gutting fish.

Needing to unload on someone, she phoned her mother, but afterwards wished she hadn't.

'Well, it's sad, love, but you knew it was just a holiday infatuation, didn't you? I mean, you told me he never called, even though he promised, and you didn't really know him, dear. I wished you'd told me you were going down there, I would have suggested it wasn't a good idea.'

The very reason she hadn't told her mother, of course.

Stephanie searched the old haunts until she found a couple of Tass's mates by the pier. They recognised her, and for once the quips were absent. They told her the facts, with all the bewilderment of youth – death was for the old, not someone like Tass, he of the ready wit, who could beguile a girl with his come-hither eyes, who was going to leave this small town one day because it was in his nature to do great things, to become famous.

From them she learned he'd broken the first rule of diving: don't go alone.

He'd gone alone and had died for it.

They told her that the structure had collapsed, trapping him. With his determination to live, he'd wriggled out of his damaged dive gear and hauled himself out from under the girder, only to find that it had also blocked the way out. He must have been able to see the distant halo of green sunlight through a porthole too small to exit as he involuntarily began to drag salt water into his lungs. His friends found him, hours later, but had they been there within minutes, it would have been too late.

It doesn't take long to drown.

As she had learned of his last great adventure, she wondered, how she could have been unaware that this had been going on. Surely, somehow, she should have *felt* it?

But it was clear, now, why he hadn't called: he'd died just two weeks after she'd left. During those long months of soul searching, her vital, beautiful lover had already died. There was tiny consolation in the thought that if he hadn't died, he would have surely called.

Numbly, she wandered out onto the crumbling breakwater, drank lukewarm coffee at the Lodge, and watched the fishermen at their chores, then as the day fled, found herself treading the paths she had trodden back in the summer, past the derelict lifeboat station, up onto the cliff that towered over Townsea.

The cold, grey November afternoon suited her mood. The leaden sky hung heavy with rain, dropping fitful spits lashed by a rising wind, while far below it seemed as if the rocks moved, clawing themselves out of the depths, to be dragged back under time and time again.

In the summer, the sea had been blue as the Mediterranean, the sun hot on her bare shoulders. It was hard to recall, here and now, with her short hair whipping around her face, savagely cutting at her cheeks, the sea a steel-grey undulating monster tipped with white spume.

The cliff path was narrow and muddy.

The raw power of nature tugged at her clothes, buffeting her; but she felt safe behind the cliff fence, a line of posts joined by barbed wire, festooned with sheep's wool.

To the left she could just make out the landslip, a great swathe of land that had slumped into the sea a hundred years ago, taking an old house with it. Tass had told her about it, back in the summer, how a mother had woken up in alarm, feeling the land heave, and managed to carry her two young children to safety just before the house slid away. She imagined it under the water like an ancient wreck, its tall chimneys wrapped in sea-weed, its sash-cord windows like black holes. But she knew, really, that the house had simply disintegrated over the years, broken up into a rubble of pebbles and concrete and polished sea glass.

The sea, Tass said, always claimed her own.

He'd been at one with the sea: a strong swimmer, a fisherman, a diver, a sailor – part merman, she had joked. Had the greedy sea claimed him for herself?

She shivered as the wind sucked at her clothes, tearing small lumps of earth from the edge, sending them tumbling down the sheer drop to the rocks below. Nervously, she took a step back.

She closed her eyes, leaned her head back, and imagined he stood there beside her. He would have laughed at the height, enjoyed the strength of the storm. He'd sought danger with a reckless, fearless passion, his zest for life infectious. She had hoped for more, but it had been her pleasure to belong to him for a brief moment in time, to share his hunger for life, his disregard for danger, his lust for adventure.

But she hadn't been there at his death.

No one had.

And now as the storm broke, wrapping itself fiercely around her, Tass touched her with the fingers of wind, enticing, cajoling as he had done so easily in the past.

She could almost hear him calling.

His eyes would be half-closed with amusement and desire, his lean strength would wrap around her, enfolding her, pleasuring her with deceptively gentle caresses.

Now she could face his silence by persuading herself that he had loved her in truth. Had he not died, he would have contacted her, for sure. She imagined his finger caressing the mobile as he scrolled through to her name and pressed *call. Sweet Stephanie, I need you*, he would have said, and she would have gone running to him.

Her eyes flashed open as a wall of water hit the cliff, dislodging a cascade of small stones. As she turned to head back down, the path lurched, and disappeared from beneath her feet.

Giving an astonished cry, she clawed the air and found herself grabbing something solid. The rocks tugged at her feet as they rushed away, the clatter lost in the noise of the storm.

Gasping, with fear she found herself hanging onto a wooden fencepost attached to its companions only by barbed wire. Her legs were dangling over the cliff.

Above her, a sign swung loose: Danger! Unstable cliff-edge. Keep clear!

She gave a disbelieving laugh, and pulled herself inward a few inches, then cried out in terror as more rocks tumbled, and she was shunted further towards the drop.

Gone was the gauze-softened image of the Tass she recalled, replaced by the horrific reality of joining him, unintentionally. Thunder crashed, the sea thrashed, and she hung on, afraid to move her grip, afraid to try to claw her way up, in case the barbed wire failed, sending her smashing onto the rocks below.

'Tass!'

She wailed his name like a prayer.

As if the prayer had been answered she felt a hand grip tightly around one of her wrists.

'Climb up,' a man's voice yelled. 'I've got you.'

She didn't dare open her eyes.

'I can't,' she gasped.

'Yes, you can. Grab my sleeve with your left hand. It's strong. It will hold.'

His hand tightened on her wrist, pulling her in a couple of inches.

She took a breath, let go of the post and clawed in panic for his arm, and clutched a handful of fabric. He pulled her another six inches.

'Good girl. Nearly there. Now, get your knees under you. That's it. Now crawl.'

The calm voice persuaded her frozen muscles to work, and as she found purchase, she was hauled forward from the edge in a slithering rush.

For a moment she and her unknown rescuer were in a tangle of limbs on the grass, then he was on his feet, pulling her up by her wrist.

'Get up,' he yelled. 'The rest might go.'

Then she was on her feet and they were stumbling, hand in hand, eyes down, blinded by the stinging rain, sliding on the loose rocks.

Eventually, the side of the life-guard station loomed through the rain, its dingy, yellow paint peeling, the fabric of the building cracked like jagged lightening from top to bottom. They ducked beneath the broken lintel, distanced suddenly from the storm which raged on outside.

Tears now came in gulping hysteria, fear of falling, fear of dying. But her saviour didn't comfort her. He took her by the shoulders, and angry words finally penetrated her gasping panic, the aftermath of something that couldn't possibly really have happened, a nightmare that would surely haunt her from now till the day she died.

'What the hell were you doing, Stephanie?'

It was late afternoon, but the light was almost gone, and his face was indistinct. 'Tass is dead, girl, and he's not coming back, and throwing yourself after him isn't going to change the fact.'

His anger seemed to drain.

'Are you all right?'

She nodded, blankly.

He gave a long, whistling sigh. 'I thought you'd gone over, and I wasn't close enough to stop you. Didn't you hear me yelling at you to come down?'

'No.'

She'd thought it had been Tass calling her.

'I saw you head up there, so I ran, but – Jesus wept, girl, you scared me. I thought we were going to be collecting your body with the lifeboat.'

'I scared me, too,' she said.

Her breathing was slowing now.

'I went up there in the summer, I had no idea...'

'The cliff goes a bit more each year. I thought you knew it wasn't safe. We were just waiting for a dry spell before we could go up and move the fence inland a bit. There were notices at the bottom of the path.'

'I didn't see them.'

'I thought you'd jumped.'

'You thought I was suicidal?' She paused, considering the possibility. No, not even for Tass. 'It was an accident.'

'I'm relieved to hear it.'

They were in the lea of the wind, but still exposed. She began to shiver, and wasn't sure whether it was from the cold, or shock.

Something else penetrated her awareness.

'I don't understand. You know me?'

When he spoke again his voice was slightly less harsh. 'I'm Rory. We met in the summer.'

She felt bad that she didn't recall him. Vaguely a face swam into view, but there had been many faces, and it had been such a short time.

'I saw you on the sea-front,' he said. 'By the time I'd parked, you were gone. I guessed you might have come up here,' he indicated their drab surroundings, and warmth flooded her cheeks.

Memories of summer nights, watching the lights of the sea-town below them reflected on the still sea along the breakwater; memories of illicit loving in the abandoned building. How did this man know?

'I just came here to remember,' she whispered. 'I didn't intend to – throw myself. It just seemed as if the sea was calling me.'

She thought he was going to laugh, but he didn't.

'The sea can have that effect. I've felt her calling before now.'

Unexpectedly he pulled her into his arms. He was a big man, and her head nestled into the crook of his shoulder.

'Cry if you need to, baby. Tass is dead, and nothing can make it better.'

His hand rested on the back of her head, stroking, comforting, as one would a child.

Now, she cried.

Earlier, she'd been alone. There had been no-one to share this grief with. Without Tass standing behind her in his cut-offs and torn T-shirt, exchanging good-natured banter with them, she was a stranger to his friends.

Yet now, after brushing with death, she stood in the abandoned life-station on the cliff, accepting the comfort of a stranger who understood.

His wet clothes smelled of oil, and he had the working-man's rock-solid strength behind the old clothes. Embarrassed, she pushed away.

He peered through the drunken door.

'It's not going to stop. Not for a while. We can't get much wetter, I guess. May as well get back to town and warm up.'

He held his hand out, and in the storm-light she caught the glimpse of a sympathetic smile. Tass, with youthful exuberance, had revelled in challenging the elements, but she thought this man probably respected them.

She took his hand. Out in the storm, the lashing rain blinded her momentarily; but they slithered down the short, slick concrete path to the road. Water dripped from her nose as they emerged onto the esplanade and sheltered under an awning. Rory wiped his face with the back of his hand.

'Where to?'

Stephanie was at a loss.

'My car's behind the boatsheds.'

'I know. I meant, where are you staying?'

'I didn't book anywhere. I'll have to find a place, or maybe just drive on home.'

She flushed slightly. He must have guessed she'd been wondering whether she could stay with Tass.

He gave her a level look.

'Come and dry off at my place. Most of the hotels and B&Bs are closed, and you're shivering.'

There was no room for argument; she was frozen. Winter was fairly upon them, the warmth of summer no more than a memory. The trees were bare, the rain bitter. He drew her towards the river-mouth, past some squat cottages, and up some wooden steps to a shanty-town building. A small sign flapped over the door: Boatbuilder.

'You live here?' Stephanie asked, her teeth chattering.

'When I'm working.'

He pulled a key from under the mat, then they were inside. The door closed onto a profound silence. In the sudden glare of electric light, Stephanie saw him for the first time, and felt embarrassed. He was a rugged man with the build of a rugby player, and a mop of sandy hair. He seemed kind enough, but she was daunted by his size.

'I shouldn't be here...'

'You can't go anywhere. You're soaked and suffering from shock. If you're worried about... I have no, ah, intentions.'

The rain had plastered his hair down broad cheeks rimmed with the fine lines of someone who continually creased his eyes against the sun. Pale blue eyes fastened on her, eye-lashes heavy with droplets of water; a weathered face, young and old at the same time.

His clothes, too, were those of a worker - oiled jumper, cotton trousers seamed with grease, all dark and colourless. But he didn't need clothes to make him, she thought. Strength and confidence emanated from him. To rescue a girl about to throw herself from the cliff had probably been no more than another day in his life. He'd mentioned the lifeboat as if he would have been one of the men manning it.

She didn't doubt it for a moment.

And if he hadn't followed her up the path, she would have been just another tragedy for the folk to talk about, she supposed, and shuddered at the recollection of the empty space that had been waiting for her.

She flushed, realising that he was staring at her with as much interest as she was staring at him. Did he see a mousy-haired, bedraggled woman slightly on the full side, mooning over a lost chance?

She felt inadequate and ugly.

He reached for a towel, and threw it at her. 'Go and stand by the Rayburn, I'll find you something dry to put on.'

The heat from the stove made her steam as she obediently rubbed the towel vigorously around her hair and face. When he came back through the open-slatted door he was dressed in clean, dry clothes: jeans that strained over the power of his thighs, and a sweatshirt which did nothing to hide the sheer width of his shoulders. No wonder he'd hauled her from the cliff edge with such ease.

He threw a large hoodie at her, and a faint smile lit his eyes.

'That should be decent on you. Give me your clothes, I'll dry them off.'

He turned and began to fuss with a kettle. After a moment's hesitation, Stephanie stripped off her top clothes and donned the hoodie. He turned to assess her. It came down to her knees.

'Take your jeans off, sit in the chair, and put the throw around you.'

Drained of will, it was so easy to do as she was told, and comforting, too. As he made large mugs of tea, he moved around the shack with economy and ease, his large hands deftly wielding the domestic implements.

He placed the mug in her hands, wrapping her fingers around it as if she wasn't capable of doing it herself. Then he spread her clothes on a rack above the Rayburn – obviously there for that purpose – and lowered it until the legs of her jeans were a few inches from the metal plate, which hissed and spattered as drops of water began to fall.

There was a strange apathy about her as she sat and reflected. Her mind had been filled with anger, against who or what she didn't know. It just wasn't *fair*. Tass was too young to be *dead*.

Her mind was floating.

She was somehow wrapped in a cocoon of warmth in this shed-like room, which was too big to be called a bedsit. Moving was an effort too great to contemplate.

Rory gazed at her, as if wondering what kind of fish he'd hauled in from the sea, but there was no pressure, and he asked no questions. Eventually he began to prepare something to eat, on a small electric hotplate on the workbench, and Stephanie found herself drifting from stunned listlessness into sleep.

Nearly falling off a cliff was way out of reach. It was a dream-time ago.

When she awoke at the simple weight of a hand on her shoulder, there was no confusion, no moment of disorientation. Tass's death had been there in her sleep, waiting for her.

She accepted the bowl of beans and mash, forking them into her mouth mechanically before succumbing once more to the strange lethargy that filled her mind.

Chapter 2

Stephanie awoke the following morning to the confusing memory that she'd allowed a stranger to take her back to his house, feed her, and put her to bed, and that it felt right.

She stretched and glanced around the small wooden room, and sleep fled. It was his room. She was also wearing one of his shirts. The intimacy of that revelation now startled her. Last night she'd been aware of little save the overwhelming confusion of weariness – she had blanked out reality and done as he had told her like a bewildered child.

She found herself lying on a narrow bunk that had been built in amongst cupboard units, for all the world like the cabin of a boat. On one wall was a faded picture of an old fisherman, his arm resting on the shoulders of a keen-eyed boy. There was a kite hanging from the ceiling, once brightly coloured, now dark with age and dust. Beside it hung a home-made model aeroplane, its green paint peeling. In one corner was a carved rocking chair, and on the windowsill was a collection of sea debris – bits of polished glass, shells, and coloured pebbles.

Other than that, it was a tidy room, functional, and personal. It betrayed – more clearly than words – the character of the man who usually inhabited it: meticulous, thoughtful, caring, and single.

That he'd let her use his room was a privilege not lightly accorded, she thought. She slid from the bed and slipped on the hoodie he'd given her last night. The air was chill on her bare legs.

She pulled back faded floral curtains.

The tiny, salt-splattered window looked out over the river basin with its meagre complement of yachts lying stranded on their moorings by a half-tide. Around the edge of the basin black mud rose to a carved bank of coarse grass above which seagulls wheeled.

She turned to a faint knock on the door.

'It's alright, I'm awake.'

She shivered as a blast of air came in with Rory. She wrapped her arms around her body.

He was fully dressed in jeans and a thick, cabled sweater, and a faint smile accompanied the steaming mug of tea.

'You'd better get back in bed before you freeze. I'll stoke up the Rayburn.'

Stephanie jumped back into the bunk and snuggled into the duvet. She had to push the sleeves of his shirt back from her hands before she could accept the mug. She flushed faintly as she muttered her thanks.

His eyes swept her blandly, but she knew he hadn't missed her embarrassment.

'Did you sleep well?'

'Like a log,' she admitted.

'Good.' He was business-like and blunt. 'My father used to say *there's nothing like sleep to heal wounds*. Reckon he was right.'

He rattled the firebox open and threw in a firelighter and some wood. He reached up to the rack.

'It'll warm up pretty quickly, now. Your clothes are dry, anyway. I'll just fetch in some more wood.'

Stephanie drew her knees up to her chest and hugged the mug. Sleep to heal wounds. Tass's death was exactly that, an open wound festering in the silence of her mind. She sipped at the tea, trying to focus her mind, but when he came back in, her fingers were clutched around the china, her face glazed.

'Don't bottle it up,' he said. 'If you need to, let it out.'

And that was all she needed for her shock and grief to pour out in gulping sobs.

He took the mug from her hand and

handed her a roll of paper tissue. She found herself dripping into a paper tissue while Rory waited patiently, his lips tight with compassion.

'I'm sorry,' she said, finally.

He shrugged. 'It's not every day you learn that someone you knew intimately died in a rather frightening way.'

Stephanie was faintly taken-aback by the bluntness of his speech. Her mother would have said *passed away*, and her father, had he been still alive, would have avoided the subject entirely.

'It seems crazy that I didn't know.'

'There's no way you could have known. It makes it worse, though to have gone on with your daily life, unaware that something so big had happened. You go back in your mind over the days and remember every joke that you laughed at, every simple little thing that upset you, and all the time this great trauma was happening and you didn't know about it. It makes you angry when you realise.'

'You sound as though you know what you're talking about.'

'I lost someone not too long ago.'

She wanted to ask, but she guessed he wasn't the kind to unload personal grief on a stranger, unlike herself.

'It's hard when there's no proof – only

what people tell you,' he added. 'It's as if they're playing a macabre joke on you. No body to look at, so you can say, yes, I can see he's dead.'

Rory's broad and weathered face had the distant honesty of a rock in an uncertain sea. As opposite to Tass as a man could be, and yet the hint of a memory was surfacing, of Rory being there with them in the pub, driving the dive boat, driving them home one evening in a big truck, the boys bouncing around in the back, larking about.

How could she have forgotten?

But she'd been focused, and probably besotted, she realised. She hoped she hadn't come across as too much of a fool.

Rory was being candid and open, in a slow West Country way. She recognised sympathy peeping from behind the blunt honesty, and understood he wasn't the kind to stoop to platitudes and sentimentality. He returned her stare with a quizzical expression, raised eyebrows, then stood up.

'I'm sorry, there's no shower here. I'll leave you to get dressed. Give me a shout when you're ready, and I'll come and put some bacon on the stove. Then we can decide what to do.'

'Do?'

Stephanie frowned. What could they do?

His bulk filled the doorway as he turned back.

'You'll want to visit his grave. We can get some flowers at the garage if you like.'

'Oh. Oh, yes,' she faltered, as the door closed.

But it hadn't occurred to her that Tass would have a grave.

Once dressed, Stephanie felt her normal self-possession take control. It would be sensible to leave straight away, but Rory had been right. She should visit the grave, if just to see his name there, and mentally say goodbye. She found her bag and rummaged in it for a brush, which she dragged hastily through her muddy, matted hair.

When she was ready she looked out of the door.

Rory was leaning against the side of his vehicle, ruddy in the biting wind. Seeing her, he heaved up a basket of logs and brought it in.

'Cold out,' he said.

Soon bacon was sizzling in a pan on the Rayburn.

'I, ah, I think I had your bed last night.'

'You did.'

'I didn't mean to put you out. You didn't sleep in the car, did you?'

'No, I bunked in Mary Jane, outside.' He smiled. 'I wasn't being crude. That's my yacht.'

He stirred the bacon, then glanced over his shoulder. 'How do you like your eggs?'

'Soft, please,' Stephanie said. 'I...'

She could tell by the set of his shoulders that he was listening. It came out in a rush.

'You saved my life last night. I just wanted to thank you.'

The shoulders lifted fractionally and dropped.

'Life is too precious to throw away. I'd have done it for anybody.'

He wasn't joking, either.

Stephanie remembered how the cliff-edge had disintegrated beneath her feet. She realised he'd put himself at risk of going the same way, leaning towards the crumbling cliff-edge, one hand grasping a fence post slightly less rotten than the one she'd managed to snag.

And she was almost a stranger to him.

Almost a stranger, because last night he'd used her name. Even though she hadn't remembered him, he'd known who she was.

He slid the bacon and eggs onto plates, liberally smothered the toast with butter, and slapped the two plates down on the small table.

'Tuck in, Stephanie, girl,' he invited.

She liked the way he said *girl*. It offered companionship without being an endearment.

To her surprise, she was famished. 'I feel a bit guilty for eating, when Tass is dead, as though I shouldn't be enjoying it.'

He raised a brow. 'That's fairly daft. 'No point pining away. Won't bring him back.'

'No, it won't. But it's how I feel.'

When he'd finished, Rory leaned his chair back on two legs, and clasped his hands behind his head.

Stephanie felt a small grin emerge at his evident satisfaction. She couldn't imagine him daintily sipping at an espresso and watching his calories.

His own grin dawned in echo of hers, and she realised with shock that he was, in fact, much younger than she had at first supposed. No more than thirty, thirty-five, perhaps. Not much older than herself. Unconsciously, she'd been comparing his brawny strength with Tass's lean and hungry vitality, and assuming he was a lot older.

Stephanie pushed her plate aside.

'I feel that saying thank you isn't enough, but there isn't anything else I can offer.'

He leaned over the table, took her hand and enclosed it in his own. 'There's something you can do for me.'

'There is?'

'Trust me.'

'Trust you for what?'

A slow smile dawned. 'I saved your life. You either trust me or you don't. I want you to promise me something.'

'Promise what?'

'Say yes, you promise, then I'll tell you.'

She nodded fractionally.

'Then, you've just become the lucky tenant of a holiday cottage in Townsea until I say you can leave.'

Stephanie stared at him blankly.

'I can't do that.'

'Why not?'

'I haven't any holiday left,' she said, bewildered. 'And I haven't any clothes, or anything.'

'You promised.'

'I know, but –'

'A promise is a promise. No buts. You owe me.'

Exasperation flared. 'I'd lose my job!'

He shrugged. 'If your firm is prepared to sack you when you're grieving, you really don't want to work there.'

'But, I, ah, damn it, why would you want me to do that?'

'To give me a chance to seduce you?'

She gave a shocked laugh. 'You're joking.'

'Of course, I'm joking. We just had to get that out of the way. I want to help you come to terms with Tass's death, because you can't do it alone. If you walk away now it will be like a canker, eating away inside you.'

'But I really don't see what you can do.'

'Just support you. Who else is going to?'

She was silent.

'All I ask is that you stop here for a while. This is where you knew him. This is where he died. If you go home now, it will fester.'

'I'm not that weak.' Her voice was dry.

'Has anyone died on you before?'

She bit her lip. 'My Dad, but it was expected. He'd been ill for a long time.'

'You loved him?'

She nodded.

'Difficult enough to cope with, even when you're expecting it, but there's something about a violent sudden death, especially of someone young. It haunts you long after you think you have it under control.'

'You sound as if you have personal experience.'

His answer was evasive. 'Living here, I've seen death enough. I'm a lifeboat volunteer, and we've saved quite a few people. I've also pulled bodies out of the water, people who got into difficulties, and died as a result; and there were some who didn't want to be saved. I've seen people cope and I've seen others go to pieces. The ones who have the strength to confront their loss cope better than those who hide their faces or walk away. So, will you stay? For a while?'

After a long pause, Stephanie admitted, 'I don't think Tass cared for me. I think I was chasing a dream.'

'And yet you still came back to find him.'

Her cheeks grew warm, and she looked away. 'I'd never met anyone like him before. It was exciting. He was attractive and attentive. No-one like that had ever shown any interest in me before. Does that sound stupid?'

'No, it sounds very honest.'

'I don't even know if I loved him.'

'Maybe none of us truly know that about the partners we choose.'

She was startled. 'Surely, we should?'

'Maybe in the end. But that first flush of love can be self-delusional. It's what happens when it wears off that matters. We hope each new and exciting relationship is going to lead to something magical and forever, but more often it ends in the reality of disappointment. We tend to blind ourselves a little with our own needs.'

He paused, his thoughts elsewhere, then he

focused back onto her. 'But that doesn't stop you from grieving for the loss. Nor should it. You didn't have time to really discover whether you loved Tass, or whether he could love you, and now you never will. In his mind he might not have been yours, but in your mind?'

Stephanie's silence was answer enough.

He reached over and took her hand.

'Stay and face it, Stephanie. For yourself; not for me or anyone else.'

Stephanie looked down and the strong, calloused hand which engulfed hers.

'How long for? How will you know when I've come to terms with his death? *Why* would you know that?'

'I won't, you will. At some stage you'll know, and tell me.'

'And then you'll release me from a crazy promise?'

'You're not being coerced. The only person who can honour a crazy promise is the person who made it.'

Stephanie whistled softly through her teeth, a self-derogatory sound. 'OK. I don't know why, but I'll stay. I must drive home and get some clothes, though.'

'If you go home you won't come back.'

'I will.'

He nodded. 'Your choice. I'll be here.'

Stephanie lived a three-hour drive inland, but somehow the hours disappeared. When she parked outside the flat she shared with Rachel, she couldn't remember driving the miles in between.

Rachel wasn't there.

As it was Sunday, she was probably with her boyfriend, whichever one it was at the moment. In a way that made it both more difficult and much easier. She'd been looking to Rachel to dissuade her from returning to Townsea, but without her there she didn't have to explain about Rory and a promise that seemed ludicrous in hindsight. Rachel would never believe his motives were disinterested. But then, honesty and integrity weren't things Rachel was too hot on, particularly in relationships.

Stephanie wrote a brief note explaining about Tass's death, and that she needed some time to get used to the idea. With it she enclosed a letter for her boss, and asked Rachel if she would get it to him, then packed, and returned to her car.

The job was dead-end, anyway; office work that took no particular skills, and left her feeling tired and frustrated at the end of each week. If she got sacked, so be it. There were plenty of other dead-end jobs around.

The thought was strangely liberating.

And maybe that's why she'd been so taken with Tass. He'd lifted the long frustration of being with people she didn't always like, both in work and out of it. He'd seen her, thrown her a life-line, and she'd latched on to it because she'd needed to. Neither of them had realised, then, that he'd been her Romeo, her tragedy in the making.

The day was miserable and cold, the storm still fretfully vandalising the countryside. Broken branches and dead leaves littered the narrow roads leading back to Townsea, and the high banks were slick with runnels of water seeping from waterlogged fields.

She was exhausted, having spent most of the day driving. She drove straight to the boatyard and parked her car near an old pick-up by the boat-shed Rory lived in. She hesitated for a moment before climbing the couple of steps to the door.

Doubt rushed in.

What if he regretted his impulse? Whose cottage had he commandeered? Who was going to pay for it? But when she knocked there was no answer.

Returning to her car she grabbed a waterproof jacket, thrust her hands into the pockets against the damp bite in the air, and set off down the mud-puddled yard.

It was bigger than she had at first supposed, filled with a variety of craft, some of which had no business being anywhere near water. Stephanie smiled fractionally at the rotting remains of a flat-bottomed punt. Some people just couldn't throw anything away. Rory, or whoever owned this yard obviously kept some of this stuff for purely sentimental reasons.

After rounding a ramshackle litter of sheds in varying states of decay, she found Rory within a makeshift corrugated winch-shed. From it a metal track slid down into the estuary; obviously the very basic means used to haul boats out for repair.

He had a mask on his face and was sanding down a new area of wood inserted cleanly into the side of a clinker-built fishing vessel. His short curly hair was white with saw dust, aging him instantly.

She watched, unnoticed.

There was something wholesome about his solitude, and his single-minded dedication. From time to time he lifted the sander and smoothed his hand along the joint, feeling for blemishes too small for the eye to perceive, then the sander would drop again and scream into action. Stephanie stood in the dying wind, hunched against the sharp salt sea breeze.

Then, as if he felt eyes on him, Rory stopped, and turned his head. Over the mask his eyes narrowed with sudden realisation, and something else which was hidden instantly. He lay the sander down by the seemingly hodgepodge of blocks and wedges that held the tons of vessel upright.

He hadn't been sure of her, despite the promise.

'I'll just pack up and be right with you,' he said.

'You don't have to stop for me.'

'The light's gone. I was finished anyway.'

He gave a fleeting grin and patted the boat almost tenderly.

'Tomorrow I can begin to varnish. She'll soon be back in the water where she belongs.'

He packed up his tools and gave the repair a final satisfied pat before leaving. They walked together back up to the hut, Rory carrying the heavy, metal tool-case with deceptive ease.

'You enjoy your work.'

'Fisher-folk don't know the meaning of the word. Fixing boats and nets is just part of life.'

His glance took the sting from the words.

'Are you fisher-folk?'

'Originally my family was. My great-grandfather set up the boat-yard after the war. He lost a leg and couldn't fish anymore. Gramps took it on, then when he died, my father took it over.'

There was pride in his voice.

'We've owned this land for upwards of seventy years, now.'

'Did you ever want to do anything different?'

He stopped and looked around.

'We all have dreams,' he said. 'But for the most part, I'm happy. There's nothing else I want desperately enough to leave this for. Do you enjoy your work?'

Stephanie shrugged.

'I work in an office. It's a job. I never grew up with any burning ambition that has been foiled, or anything like that. I'm not *unhappy* with the way things are.'

'But not fulfilled, either?

'Maybe.'

'Is that why you came here in the summer?'

'If you mean did I come looking for a stud, absolutely not. I came to be by the sea; to get my feet wet. To dive or sail. The holiday romance was unintentional.'

They walked up the steps, and Rory opened the door for her.

'Yet you were pretty good out on the boat, I recall.'

'My Dad used to have a dingy when I was small, so we sailed a bit, mostly on a reservoir near my home. That stopped when he died. Mum wasn't interested. I thought I'd take it up when I'd finished school, but I came home one day, and the dingy was gone. She didn't realise I wanted it, and I'd just assumed I'd end up with it. It was a bit of a leveller.'

Inside Rory's cabin, the Rayburn was belting out heat. Stephanie felt her cheeks begin to tingle.

'And you met Tass through the dive school?'

'Yes. I got into diving by accident a couple of years back, and loved it. I belong to a club down the coast a bit. I've been wanting to dive the wrecks in this bay for a while.'

'Inevitable, I guess.'

Tass had told her that in the height of summer he made his way by escorting trips – fishing, diving, climbing, and sailing – then in the autumn he would have been off delivering rich men's yachts back for overwintering in their home-ports. He'd never had full time employment. That wasn't who he was, he'd stated proudly.

'The cottage is a mile outside town,' Rory told her, breaking into her reverie. He dumped his gear and collected a bunch of keys from a hook.

'Did you bring anything to eat?'

Stephanie shook her head. It hadn't occurred to her.

'Follow the pickup. We'll stop at the garage shop, then you can follow me out to the cottage.'

She followed along the empty esplanade. Beyond, the sea was grey and choppy, the sky fitful.

The lady in the tiny supermarket by the garage gave a quick glance at Rory's bland face, seeing them shopping together, lightly fished for information. 'Hullo, dear. I remember you from the summer, of course, but I can't recall your name?'

'Stephanie.'

'Oh, yes. You were with Tass, then, weren't you? Such a sad business. Him so young, too.'

'Tragic,' she agreed. 'But I'm not *with* Rory.'

There was a tinkle of false laughter. 'Oh, my dear, I think you misunderstood.'

'I don't think I did,' Stephanie said in annoyance, when they were outside.

'No. By tomorrow it will be all over the town that you're staying at Highview,' Rory said with a grimace after they left. 'I didn't think about that, or I would have got some shopping in earlier. You'll just have to take it on the chin. There's little enough to keep people going through the winter here, except gossip.'

Stephanie shrugged. 'They can say what they like. I doubt I'll come back here again.'

She regretted returning already. Rory's kindness was almost an embarrassment, making her feel inadequate. She wondered if he now regretted his compassionate impulse. She would stay for just a day or so, she decided. Go and see Tass's grave, offer her condolences to his uncle, though she had never met him she felt that she ought to, then tell Rory she was quite happy to leave, she was over it.

Strangely, it did feel like that already.

Tass was diminishing to an old sepia photograph in the back of her mind. Scarcely real, barely known. She was amazed at herself for coming back at all, looking for him, when he'd obviously forgotten about her the moment she left. The dawning awareness that she truly had been nothing more than a holiday lay for him made her feel slightly dirty.

The holiday cottage was the end one of three, situated in its own drive, half way up the side of the river valley. She parked her car beside the pickup and followed Rory to the front door. He insisted on carrying her case.

All the cottages looked sadly neglected.

The whitewashed stone walls were grey with mould. The front door was made of dark oak which had warped or shrunk. Inside the front door was a tired velvet drape to keep out the drafts. The rooms were tiny, with frames that had the quaint, appearance of age, and were certainly not double-glazed.

She dumped her handbag on a sofa, thinking it was a sad end to a house that had once been a home. From the main living room window, she could see little of the new town, and few cars; but the fishing boats, bobbing within the circular protection of the sea wall, pulled her into a curious time-warp.

'It's lovely, isn't it?' Rory said softly from just behind her. 'Like stepping back in time. An illusion of peace and tranquillity, as if modern life hasn't yet intruded. It's easy to forget that in those days the poor starved in winter, their children died of unknown ailments, and the men still had to take the boats out in the face of a gale.'

She wondered how he knew she was thinking of the past.

'They used to put candles in the upstairs windows of these cottages to welcome the returning fishermen home. Sometimes the candles would burn a long time in hope.'

'That's so sad.'

'But real somehow. People today live in their insular pockets, watching television, working Monday to Friday, shopping on Saturday, and go to the garden centre on Sunday.'

'You make it sound almost sordid.'

'No, *that's* sad – that they've forgotten what it is to be alive. Come on, I'll show you upstairs.'

The stairs were steep and narrow, and the three bedrooms half in the roof space, the window sills were mere inches from the floor, and there were small gables above. Rory had to bend to go through the doorway. 'I'll put your stuff in here,' he said. 'This room is the best because you can lie in bed and see the sea, but you can move it if you want.'

Despite the dilapidation, the cottage didn't have the seediness of a holiday cottage.

'Someone lives here,' Stephanie said, looking around at the homeliness, the pictures, the small personal items.

'Yes. A friend of mine. It's not rented out, except to friends, but he's away at the moment.'

'Won't he mind me using it? He's not likely to come back unexpectedly, is he?'

Rory shook his head. 'No on both counts.'

He led the way back downstairs, and showed her the kitchen, which was a new building tacked on to the back of the house, and presumably it was insulated and double glazed, being on the north face.

'I'd stay and make something for dinner, but I actually have a prior engagement for tonight.'

He wrote on a pad.

'That's my mobile. If you need me call at any time, do; and I mean that. Otherwise, I'll call and collect you at ten tomorrow.'

Stephanie was glad he was going.

His overpowering presence filled the tiny cottage. She pressed fingers to her temple at the onset of a headache which had been threatening. It was all too much, somehow.

'You don't have to. I can manage, really.'

'I want to.'

'Thank you.'

It came out rather grudgingly, Stephanie felt, but she was too weary to care. It was his own fault for being so helpful. She'd discovered, herself, that sometimes, being overly helpful backfired.

He didn't take offense, though. He just gave her the fleeting hint of a smile before disappearing. She heard the sound of his pick-up in her mind long after it was out of earshot, then the silence became oppressive.

She unpacked the groceries, made herself a cup of tea, and went to sit in an armchair which was placed by the living room window. Staring out sightlessly over the darkened landscape a vast unhappiness welled within her which had no concrete point of origin.

What on earth was she doing here?

She felt immensely sorry for herself. Deeper than her present displaced disorientation, deeper than her elusive dreams of Tass, unhappiness welled into rasping grief which forced itself noisily from her throat. She folded on the chair and cried harder than she had ever remembered, and it was all his fault. If he hadn't made her come here, she could have talked to Rachel about Tass, and surely that would have been better than this sense of emptiness?

Several times she reached for the phone, but each time she drew her hand back, and each time she cried with frustration. If crying was therapy, she was going to get over this exceedingly quickly.

She discovered a text message in her phone from Rachel asking what the hell she was doing, this seedy-sounding Rory person could be a murdering rapist.

She sent a message straight back saying she was fine, in a cottage on her own, and please don't worry; she knew what she was doing.

Except she didn't, and they both knew it.

Rachel's comment slightly irritated her, though. Rory was no seedy rapist, of that she was certain. He was a kind person, trying to do a kind deed. He didn't pull his punches, and wasn't afraid to make the odd wisecrack. She liked that. Whether it was sensible, or the right thing to do, well, that was another matter.

She couldn't phone her mother, either, because her mother would panic, and try to persuade her to come home.

She should just climb back in her car and make the trip back home again, but she was too tired, and, she suspected Rory was half expecting her to do that.

Maybe that was why he'd left her so quickly, leaving her options open. She was almost sure that if she drove back into town she'd find Rory on his own at the boatshed. Ten to one he didn't have a prior engagement at all, he was simply giving her the chance to turn tail and run.

It was that, more than anything, that made her finally knock up a ham sandwich, make a cup of tea, veg in front of a soap on TV, then haul herself up to the bedroom he'd suggested.

Tomorrow things would be much clearer.

She hoped.

Chapter 3

The mirror showed Stephanie just how badly she'd slept, and there wasn't a lot she could do to disguise the fact. When Rory came she still looked pale, her eyes washed-out, red-rimmed and swollen, her curly cloud of mousy hair lank, in spite of brushing.

And there she was, sitting by the window, like the fisherman's wife of old, waiting for a man who would never come because he was dead. The sea had made a sailor's widow of her before she had ever been married.

Her ears pricked up at the sound of Rory's battered truck climbing the steep hill, and she stood reluctantly.

Today she had to face the grave, and he was there to make sure she did it; for all the world like a doctor - take your medicine like a good little girl, it will make you much better. And yet, when she opened the door to him, she was relieved she didn't have to face it on her own.

Rory was looking fresh and rested, damn

him, and quite presentable. The fisherman's jersey and working boots had been replaced by clean casual clothes. He brushed up well, she had to admit. When his keen eyes assessed her, he didn't ask how she had slept.

'Ready?'

'As ready as I'll ever be.'

He drove in silence down to the town, and a faint drizzle spat at the windscreen, making it necessary to use the wipers, which scraped with teeth-shuddering squeals against the glass.

The pick-up was old, and noisy, the seats torn; very much a working vehicle.

They trundled slowly past the painted hotels, around the roundabout near the cob, and on up the other side of the hill. The church was set back from the road, a miserable grey stone building with no redeeming features, surrounded by an army of lichen-covered stones.

He parked outside the lychgate and held it open for her to pass through. This side, at the front of the church the gravestones were all old, the angels and marble slabs liberally desecrated by seagulls, but as they walked around the side there was an area where new graves had been decorated with wilting cut blooms.

'I didn't bring any flowers,' Stephanie said.

'If you'd felt it was necessary you would have remembered,' he said calmly.

Stephanie thought Tass would have laughed.

Get away! Flowers are for old women and guilty husbands!

He led her to a plain stone. For a moment she didn't want to look, then when she did, she felt nothing at all. It was the grave of a stranger. *William Purdie, twenty-four years,* it stated. *Died in the arms of his mistress, the sea.*

She frowned.

'I didn't know his name was William.'

'He was always called Tass, ever since I remember. I don't recall why, but he was Christened William, after his grandfather.'

She was vaguely annoyed that Rory knew more about Tass than she did.

'Who thought of the inscription?'

'His uncle.'

'It's weird.'

She stood there with her lack of feeling and her disorganised jumble of thoughts.

'Why did they bury him? I'm sure he said he'd wanted to be cremated.'

'You talked about that kind of stuff?'

'Oh, there was a crowd of us. I remember he said he had a morbid hatred of graveyards.'

'Well, perhaps Thomas didn't know that. The Purdies have always been buried here.'

'He would have hated it.'

'Tass isn't in that body anymore, Stephanie. It's an empty shell. Don't think of it. Whether he was buried or cremated, if he had a soul it's out there in the sea somewhere, riding on the white horses, breaking on the pebbles, laughing in the spume. He finally achieved that freedom he sought so avidly.'

Stephanie felt numb. The grave was distant, unreal. She'd vaguely supposed the sight of it would sadden her, but it didn't. There was no way Tass could be lying beneath that cold earth.

'Have you ever been in the church?'

She shook her head. He took her hand and pulled her. 'Come, I want to show you something.'

Inside the church it was lighter than she would have thought from its grey, unimpressive exterior. There were few coloured panels left in the windows, and few carvings to lift the cumbersome architecture, but it was not dark.

'Here,' Rory said, pausing before a brass plaque on the wall. 'Read this.'

Martin *Purdie, lived by the sea, taken by the sea, November 1890, remembered with love by his children.*

'And this one,' Rory said, dragging her on.

Martha Purdie, 1873, aged nineteen, died in a boating accident trying to save her two brothers from a sailing mishap.

'And this, and this...'

There were other names, and so many of them had been taken by the sea. So many had not lived to see old age, so many men outlived by their wives.

'It's sad,' Stephanie whispered. 'So many drowned.'

'It was a hard life, then, but no less traumatic for those who lost loved ones. But do you notice that on all the plaques there's pride?'

'Pride and love.'

'That's right.'

He put his arm around her, and she found it comforting.

'They all found something good to say about the ones they lost. When all you have left of someone is the memories, you have to bring the good memories, the happy memories to rest in the place you look in. Tass did a lot of living in his short life, a lot more than some of the others in here.'

'But there was so much he didn't do; he had such grand plans!'

'He did that. Some of us get right to the end

of our lives having achieved nothing more than dream. He meant to make his dreams happen.'

'He must have been so angry!'

'Angry for dying?' Rory smiled. 'You may well be right. He was very ambitious, and had he lived he would have made a name for himself somewhere, somehow.'

'You almost make him sound unscrupulous.'

'That wasn't my intention. Tass was a charismatic young man. He was attracted to life, and people were attracted to him because of it.'

'I should know.'

He led her back down the aisle, out into the day.

'He's been dead for five months now, Stephanie. In Townsea we're beginning to get used to the idea. Nobody had any idea you were pining for him, or that you didn't know. I'm so sorry.'

'Why should you be sorry? It wasn't your fault.'

'I should have thought of letting you know.'

'Well, you didn't really know anything about me.'

'I knew your name. With the internet today, I'd have hardly had to hire a detective.'

He was leading her back to the truck.

There, she hesitated, before saying, 'I get the feeling you didn't like Tass very much.'

He seemed to think a long time before replying.

'There were things about Tass I didn't admire.'

'His determination to get on in life?'

'Not so much that, but his lack of empathy with others. He could be devious. He was always like that, even through school. I hoped, as he grew older, that he'd mature, but now we'll never know, will we?'

'You sound like his father.'

He smiled. 'Old before my time, that's me.'

Rory opened the door, and she climbed in, folding her hands on her lap. He started the engine and reversed out into the main road, but instead of driving back through the town, he took the road on up the hill.

'Where are we going?'

He pulled into a small lay-by at the top of the hill, and said, 'We're going for a walk.'

When they pulled in to a lay by, she realised she'd been there before.

From here there was a small cliff-path sweeping down to a sheltered bay. In the summer it was mostly the locals who came here – all pebbles, and no sand, it wasn't a place which endeared itself to holiday-makers.

'I came here with Tass.'

'I know. You did a shore dive, out to the little wreck 30 yards out.' Rory slipped sideways in his seat and surveyed her. 'Are you OK?'

Her eyes flooded, and she blinked hard. 'Jesus, take your pound of flesh, why don't you.'

He smiled. It's just a bay. Come and see it now, after the storm.'

'I don't want to.'

'You want to go back to your safe little office, your safe little life? It's all right during the day, you can pretend none of this happened, you can even pretend not to remember Tass. But what of the nights? What of the memories of summer nights in the bracken on the cliffs? How many years will it take before you can sleep without the fear of him returning to haunt you?'

'Damn it,' she said in a low voice, and let the door open with a crash against the wind. She slammed it shut venomously, and marched off down the cliff path; but the dry slope of the summer had matured into a muddy slide. She sensed Rory behind her but didn't look back.

It was from this bay that she had also snorkelled with Tass, floating in their wetsuits above the swaying weed and the darting fish, hovering on the brink between sea and sky. He'd carried their gear down the cliff his shoulder, his lean strength beautiful to watch, his long, tanned legs bounding easily over the scree in spite of the awkward bulk of his load.

And they had floated side by side, listening to the sounds of the sea, just pointing as each new treasure hove into sight. Now and again they would fold and dive, struggling downwards against the buoyancy of the wetsuits, and all too soon would shoot back to the surface to spout like whales.

Then, bobbing on the sea on her back, stretched out like a starfish, she had stared up at the distant streak of cloud with Tass a mere tantalising finger-breadth away as they gasped for air.

It was on this same path he had turned and laughed up at her as she descended carefully, trying not to slip.

'Come on, Steph, go for it!' he'd yelled.

And she had, throwing caution to the winds, enjoying the brief lack of care which he lent her as she bounded after him. It hadn't been easy to let go of the city girl. But looking at the path now, she realised she wouldn't have wanted to slip. The fall would have been onto rocks and pebbles, at the minimum providing a broken arm or leg for a couple of minutes' exhilaration.

She wouldn't do that now.

Her thoughts made her unsure of herself, and her foot slipped. She gasped just fractionally, but Rory's hand was there on her elbow instantly. She shrugged herself free without offering thanks, and struggled on to the bottom.

She hadn't wanted to come here. On the faceless sea she had viewed from the esplanade there were no landmarks to trigger memories, but here the memories abounded. How could a mere two weeks have stretched into the long summer idyll that sprang to mind? It was as if Tass's death had elongated everything, magnified and altered the hours into days, the weeks into years.

At the foot of the cliff she sat down on a wet boulder and just stared out to sea, hugging the waterproof tightly around her torso. The wreck where Tass had died was further around the bay, but she shivered now with the echo of a claustrophobic memory of the wreck that had finally killed him. She had snagged her regulator on a shard of metal. It had ripped out of her mouth in a cascade of bubbles. She had panicked for a long moment trying to recover it, but Tass had reached around to calmly place it back in her mouth.

How had someone with that sheer confidence, that lack of fear, have ended up getting himself into a situation he couldn't get out of? But maybe that confidence was the very reason it happened. The confidence to get himself out of trouble hadn't taken into account the joker in the pack: the mocking hand of fate.

Back then, his hands and eyes had offered comfort as she recovered her equilibrium. Then his brows had raised in question. She'd made the OK circle of forefinger finger and thumb. He'd nodded and smiled through his regulator. He wouldn't have understood her need to return to the surface, to feel the fresh air on her face. He wouldn't have wanted to know her weakness.

They'd carried on with the dive, and she later said how great it had been, but she hadn't enjoyed it from that point on.

She shivered slightly.

'I've dived off here, too,' Rory said, reminding her of his presence.

She turned startled. 'I didn't know you dived.'

He smiled, a flash of white in the rain runnels on his face. 'I learned to dive just to fix boats, to free tangled props, and whatever. I got hooked.'

Stephanie's face softened.

'It's a different world out there,' she said. 'Like being in space. A hostile environment if you get it wrong.'

'Sure is. By like all dangerous sports, you minimise the danger by following certain codes of practice.'

And there it was again, that hint that Tass had been irresponsible. But she had to admit that his death had been his own fault. A diving buddy could have saved him. They weren't so deep, a friend could have made it to the surface without a bottle, to go for help.

'Are there good memories?' Rory asked, eventually.

She grimaced.

'Some. But the bad ones have the upper hand. I love diving, but off England it can be an unpredictable experience. A long drive sometimes, with a murky, cold sea as the end of it, and no visibility.'

'And sometimes good.'

'Yes, I dived the Manacles, off Cornwall, once. The water was so clear you could see them from the boat. That was one of my best experiences.'

'Not with Tass?'

'No, before that. I would like to dive somewhere warm one day, see the coral reefs, the blue holes, the lagoons.'

'That would be something else, that would,'

Rory agreed.

Hunched against the November blast it seemed unreal.

'Have you ever been abroad?' she asked.

'Plenty, but not for holidays. I always intended to, but somehow the boatyard always got in the way.'

'I know that feeling. Living for work, working to live.'

'That, too. But more than that, I never wanted to go abroad alone. When I go I want to have someone to share it with.'

'Tass never cared who was with him as long as he wasn't alone.'

Rory glanced at her. 'You knew that?'

She nodded. 'He needed to be, ah, admired. People warned me. I think they were being kind, but I thought, maybe...' she didn't finish.

Rory grimaced.

'Maybe you were the one? Unfortunately, his dreams of wealth and fame would have got in the way, even so.'

There it was again, Stephanie thought. That unvoiced feeling, not quite hatred, but close to it.

'Did he have other girls in the summer - after me, I mean.'

Rory's silence was her answer.

'I feel such a fool,' she said. 'If I'd come

back and seen him with someone else, perhaps by now I wouldn't care, but all the things he said to me, about how much he loved me,' her voice was low. 'They were so *real.*'

'But they were real. At that moment in time he probably did love you. He lived for the moment.'

'He asked me to stay, and I said no. I had to go back to work. If I'd stayed...'

'If you'd stayed, he would have loved you until you got in his way,' Rory said bluntly. 'Until you quite innocently stopped him from doing something, going somewhere, for whatever reason.'

Stephanie looked up into Rory's honest face.

'Why don't I hate him for that, Rory, when I know you're right?'

He sat down beside her on the cold rock.

'Love is a strange thing. No rhyme, no reason. You meet someone and, suddenly, there it is. Caring for someone beyond sense, beyond rational thought. It's like a disease. You don't know you have it until it has a good grip on your system, and by then you're too weak to fight it.'

'Have you ever loved like that?'

'Once. But it wasn't reciprocated.'

He said no more, and his attitude allowed

no room for prying.

'Did you want to fight it, to free yourself?'

'No.'

The tide was on the turn, and he reached down and picked up a newly wet pebble and hurled it passionately into the sea.

'No, I didn't want to fight it. But when your love isn't returned, you have to stand back, distance yourself, break free of it before it destroys you. I swore that I would never allow it to happen to me again.'

'That's sad.'

'It's also impossible. You can't stop your feelings any more than you can stop the tide. And what's even more difficult is stopping that frustrated love from turning to jealousy or hatred.'

'So why are you making me wallow in it, when it was probably just a passing fancy, anyway?'

He smiled.

'If you eat ice-cream until it makes you sick, you'll never want more.'

He held out his hand. 'Let's go back and get warm. We've done enough wallowing. I'm freezing.'

Stephanie shivered, and held out her hand. 'Me, too. It's the medicine that's going to kill me, not the illness.'

It was easier going back up the tiny cliff path than coming down. She pulled her hood up, faced inward, and could see the footholds, but even so, Rory insisted on going behind her in case she slipped.

'You don't have to fuss, so,' she said.

'Maybe,' he replied blandly, 'But I'm afraid I was brought up on old-fashioned values, and habits die hard.'

'Protecting the weaker sex?'

'Different,' he said. 'That you can't deny; but stronger in many ways, and us macho men would never survive without you, after all.'

Stephanie choked on a laugh, and carried on climbing. Back in the truck, she began to shiver. The insidious drizzle had seeped into her clothes. 'Shall we go back to the hut?' Rory asked. 'We'll get warmer more quickly there. The cottage has central heating, but I didn't think to turn it on.'

'OK.'

So once again she found herself huddled into a jumper that smelled of wood-smoke. He threw a slug of whiskey into a hot coffee while her clothes steamed above the Rayburn.

She was still unsure of Rory's motives.

He was being very supportive. Almost too supportive for someone he didn't really know, and about someone she was beginning to think he didn't like very much.

It was strange, too, how her mental infatuation with Tass had dissolved almost to the point she wondered why on earth she had been so focussed. Lack of self-worth? She was sure her initial grief was shock, that someone so vital had simply ceased to exist. She was sad about that, but the true realisation that she had known, deep inside, that there had been no true relationship, was a truth that his death had cruelly exposed.

She'd been kidding herself, because she'd needed the relationship more than he had. Tass had opened her eyes to a different way of life, and she wanted to get it back.

The grave she had been so scared of seeing had meant nothing, after all, it belonged to a stranger; and it seemed her rose-tinted memories meant little, either.

And yet what now? She realised she was floating in a world she knew nothing about. A world in which Rory was a key. There was something very peculiar about his determination to see her through her crisis.

She was almost scared to know.

He had a strength of character that seemed to push her from behind. He had asked for a promise, she had given it. He had indicated he thought she wouldn't keep that promise, so she had, maybe from some perverse need to prove she was reliable? But why did she care what he thought?

She had the suspicion she was being manipulated, but for what reason? Her promise was ostensibly to let him help her, but they both knew she was grieving for something that had never existed.

But, he was strong.

He'd saved her life, without doubt, but his strength was not just physical, it was an integral part of his character. He hadn't forced her to do anything. Everything she had done, she had done because he had made her understand it was the right thing to do.

But for whom?

He sat beside her on the bench by the table, gazing into some distant space within his mug of coffee, while Stephanie stared at his profile. Such a powerful face. Not handsome, but rugged, seamed against the wind, clean and as wholesome. His mouth was sensuous even in repose, and the pale eyes, hidden beneath the dropped lids with their curved lashes, saw more than was proper.

She wondered what woman had spurned the love of this gentle giant. What foolish woman had been the focus of his integrity and loyalty, and not reciprocated it? If he gave that love to a woman, she realised, it would be forever. She would never have to fear his eyes prowling the promenade, his mouth watering at the goods on display, season after season.

Then his head turned just fractionally and caught her calculating assessment. They were still for a moment, eyes locked, then Rory's head dipped just fractionally in her direction. For a fleeting moment she thought he was going to kiss her, but he stood up, and crashed out of the door.

Stephanie stared after him.

He'd been going to kiss her, of that she was sure. She was shocked to find a small tendril of disappointment filling her breast, because she'd wanted him to do just that. But it wasn't right, she knew, when she was supposed to be grieving.

The afternoon lengthened, and Rory didn't come back. Stephanie eventually began to prowl around the hut looking at his personal things: books, mementoes, and knick-knacks.

Her car was up at the cottage, and she felt slightly trapped by her reliance on him to get her back up there. She shook her head. Hell, she could call a taxi, if she wanted.

She realised she was in a state of anticipation, waiting to find out something. What, she had no idea, but he was keeping something from her. Something she needed to know, she was sure.

On one wall there was another picture of the old fisherman dressed in a pair of waders, working on some lobster pots at the side of the quay. There was something familiar in the face, in the level of concentration maybe.

She realised he must be Rory's father.

At Rory's continued absence, Stephanie rooted around by the tin sink and found some vegetables, and a few tins. In an hour it would be darkening outside, and they had missed lunch altogether. She began to throw things into a pot. When she was satisfied she dragged her cardboard-stiff jeans from the rail, hoisted herself into them, and went searching.

Rory was beneath the overhang of his working shed. She knew without words that he'd heard her come in, though he didn't look up. The patched area he'd been sanding before was now smooth with varnish, and he was cleaning the brush in a jar filled with something alcoholic.

Stephanie grimaced at the smell.

'You get used to it,' Rory said without looking up. 'The smell of grease, varnish, wood-shavings, and fish. You even get to like it after a while.'

'You must be frozen.'

'I'm used to it.'

'Do you like that too?'

He didn't miss the bite in her voice.

'There are some things in life that have to be accepted. In my line of work cold is one of them.'

Stephanie leaned against the side of the shed and crossed her arms. He cleaned the brush again thoroughly before he was satisfied, and hung it on a nail to drip, studiously not looking her way. She got the impression he'd rather she left him alone.

Well, it was his fault she was here, and he knew her car was up at the cottage.

'The fisherman in the photographs; is he your father? she asked.

'Yes. They were taken when I was about ten.'

'Does he still work from Townsea?'

'He's dead.'

Her silence was filled with a hundred questions she didn't think he'd want her to ask. He glanced over and probably saw them on her face.

'He didn't drown. He had hardening of the arteries, and a stroke almost three years ago, now, that finished him off.'

'What happened to his boat?'

'It wasn't his. The boat in the picture belongs to my Uncle. Father used to go out with Jack if he was needed, but more often he would work in the yard.'

'What about your mother?'

'She bought a flat in Cornwall. She couldn't bear to live here after he died.'

He stood up and jammed his hands in his pockets.

'I'll take you back up the hill, if you like.'

'I put a stew on the Rayburn.'

'Oh.'

'But you can have it. I don't mind.'

'Thanks.'

They walked back to the shack in silence. Stephanie collected her bag and her keys, but Rory stood by the door, almost embarrassed.

'I've been behaving like a bear. Will you share the stew with me?'

'I don't want to intrude. I feel I've become a bit of an embarrassment. You wish I wasn't here, now.'

He made a dismissive gesture, his lips pursed with indecision.

'No, of course not. It's my problem, not yours.

She smiled faintly.

Rory smiled, too, almost in self-derision.

'I didn't mean it that way.'

'I know. Your space has been invaded. I get the impression you don't bring women here.'

'I don't often bring anyone here,' he said.

He walked over to the pan, took the lid off, and sniffed. His brows rose.

'Did you make that with things you found here?'

Stephanie grinned. 'I'd have done dumplings, too, but I couldn't find any suet.'

'Damn it! I haven't had dumplings since mother left. Or a dinner that smelled like that, come to think of it.'

'So, I've found something you're not good at, have I?'

'I never said I was perfect. Anything I cook gets burned, goes lumpy, or is rock solid.'

'You live on beans and mash?'

'The Rayburn is good at those.'

He finally took his waterproof off, and seemed to shed with it his reluctance for her company.

'Would you like a beer? Or some wine?'

'A beer would be good, thanks.'

He nipped outside and came back in with a four-pack.

'It's better than a fridge outside at the moment.' He pushed the wet hair back from his forehead and sighed. 'But I wish the rain would ease up for a bit.'

Stephanie took the can and cracked it open. It hissed and dribbled onto the bare boards. 'Good job you aren't house-proud,' she said.

'I don't actually live here. Well, not all the

time.'

'No, I'm staying in your house, aren't I?'

He gave a sheepish grin. 'I thought you'd guess, but I didn't want you to think...'

'It's all right, I don't.'

'How old are you?'

'Thirty-two going on eighty. You're not supposed to ask questions like that.'

'I don't see age as a big secret. When I saw you with him, though, back in the summer, I thought you were much younger.'

'I get the feeling that's not a compliment.'

'It wasn't supposed to be an insult. You were just – so happy.'

Her brows rose. 'You really did notice me, then?'

'Yes.' He turned his back and began to riddle the Rayburn furiously. 'I noticed.'

Stephanie leaned back and watched him. He was angry again, and she didn't know why. It was as if he resented talking about her time with Tass, as if he was jealous. That was ridiculous, though. He hadn't even known her, then.

When he'd crashed the Rayburn about enough, he opened his own beer and downed half of it, lost in some private reverie, then he turned and gave her a rueful grimace.

'I'm sorry I walked out on you just now. I'm used to my own company, I'm afraid.'

'I'll go away if you want me to.'

'No. No, I'd like you to stay. It would be pretty stupid you sitting on your own up the hill, and me sitting on my own down here. Tell me something about you.'

Stephanie blinked. 'Like what?'

'What job you do, what you watch on TV.'

She grimaced. 'I'd bore you tears. My work is just work. I go in, do the job, then go home and leave it behind. I'm a PA-come-secretary. I take phone calls, type letters, file things – you know. But I love being by the sea. Or on it or under it. It was my Dad who got me interested in sailing, but I didn't do if for a long time, work and lack of incentive. It was an article in the National Geographic that got me going on diving. I saw the pictures, and it wasn't enough. I wanted to actually be there, see it for myself.'

'And what do you do in those long lonely evenings after work, on your own?'

'Am I sounding as if I don't have a social life?'

'Pretty much.'

'Oh. Well I do meet up with some friends for a drink sometimes, but mostly I read, or watch films.'

A brow rose in question. 'Read what?'

Stephanie looked vaguely embarrassed. 'Fiction. Thrillers, detective fiction, books where people *do* stuff. Even if it's a bit far-fetched.'

'Me, too. When I need an adventure, I read. It's less life-threatening to read about someone else doing dangerous stuff, and cheaper.'

She smiled. 'And that from someone who is a lifeboat volunteer?

'Did I tell you that? I don't recall. But I can't be out saving people all the time, it's exhausting.'

'I've been reading about other people's adventures since I was a child. It was only after Mum got rid of Dad's dingy that I realised I'd been intending to use it. There came a time when reading about it wasn't enough. I wanted an adventure, and I was reading a book about a man with a boat. Before I realised what I'd done, I'd committed myself to a week's sailing course.'

'On your own? That was quite brave.'

'It was daunting. I'd gone on holiday with my flat-mate, Rachel, the previous year, but she just wanted me to make up a twosome, and that got nasty at one point when she picked up two lads for us, and I wasn't up for it. Once she got herself a regular boyfriend, I was off the hook. She told me she didn't want me to go on holiday with them, I'd be a gooseberry. She thought I'd mind, but I was so relieved. Mum suggested I go to Scotland with her, but the thought of spending two weeks with a load of ageing relatives wasn't my idea of a holiday. Not that I don't like them,' she added hastily.

'Did you enjoy your sailing holiday?'

'I was terrified! It was a bad week. It rained, hailed, and I was thoroughly miserable, but the wind wasn't quite strong enough to abandon the course. If it had been, I might have left and never gone back.'

She leaned her chin on her hand reflectively.

'But in a funny way, that's what made it. It wasn't all bikinis in the sun, like the adverts. For the first time in my life I felt truly alive. I wasn't reading about it, I was doing it. While it was happening, I felt and looked like a bedraggled waif. It was only after I returned to my flat and went back to my safe little job that I realised I wanted to do it again.'

She gave him a sidelong glance. 'I suppose that sounds stupid, when you've probably grown up on boats.'

'No, it doesn't. Boats are like a love-affair. Sometimes you think you loathe them and want to leave them for ever, but you find you can't. You love them too much, and when you're away, you pine. I couldn't leave the sea now. It's in my blood.'

'You're lucky.'

He raised his brows. 'Why?'

'Because you live here. You're part of it – the fishermen, the background. I come to the coast a few times a year and go away again; a stranger, an outsider.'

'*Belonging* isn't always as straightforward as it sounds. It's even harder when you try to break the mould and do something that changes the status quo.'

'Are you?'

'I keep trying, but the mould is strong. My father wanted me to leave school and start work with him when I was sixteen, but I wouldn't. I was one of those strange kids who wanted an education. I wanted to make something of myself. Then, when he thought I was going to come home I signed on with the Navy.'

'What's wrong with that?'

He sighed.

'I didn't know Dad was ill. He never told me he, but he was hoping I'd take over. I only stayed with the Navy for a couple of years, found it didn't suit me, and came home. By then I knew Dad needed me, and the boatyard just took over. I guess I always knew it would. I was just rebelling. All kids do.'

'I got the impression you loved it.'

'Maybe I do, but it's a double-edged sword. A love-hate relationship. Sometimes I'd like to walk out and never come back, and yet I can't let go.'

Although his voice remained level, Stephanie heard desperation behind the words. She understood, without a shadow of a doubt that Rory knew great loneliness; and in spite of this he still had the time to take her under his wing and sort out her problems.

'You're a very generous man, Rory,' she said softly. 'I'll never forget what you did for me.'

He dispelled despondency with a practiced shrug of the shoulders.

'Enough of maudlin stuff. Let's have dinner.'

Stephanie smiled, but inwardly she was thinking she was not the only one who was refusing to face reality. In some ways Rory needed her at this time as much as she needed him. She wondered why he'd got to the age he had – he was surely older than her – without ending up married, with a house full of kids.

After all, she thought wistfully, he owned his own house. He'd be a good catch. Then another thought popped into her head. Maybe he was gay?

But he'd tried to kiss her, hadn't he?
Now she wasn't sure.

Chapter 4

Rory drove Stephanie back up to the cottage after dinner and wouldn't stop for a drink. He made excuses: it was late, he had work to do in the morning; but she gathered that he simply wanted to be alone, so said she was tired, too.

She wasn't lying.

They'd been together for most of the day, and even though she liked his company, liked him, the fact that they were strangers finding their way around each other had become increasingly obvious.

Later that evening Stephanie lay in bed listening to the wind lashing the rain against the window-pane, and couldn't sleep. She wondered what it must have been like, lying there waiting and hoping for a loved one to return, wondering all the time if he'd already drowned.

Almost of its own accord a tightness built up in her chest as she thought of the dark depths of the sea, being pulled under, being unable to breathe, knowing you were going to die.

She tried to imagine Tass standing at the tiller of an old fishing smack, his hands knotted with hard usage, but it didn't gel. He would have hated the sheer drudgery of fishing. What came to mind was something other: Tass at the wheel of a big modern yacht, feet spread, head thrown back, his eyes alight with savage enjoyment. That would have been where he pictured himself, in a few years, once he'd made a bit of money.

Thinking about him brought no wave of longing, just a distant pain that the sea could snuff out the bright flame of his life in moments. Because of all things, Tass had loved *living*.

Maybe he *had* disregarded his own safety as the old fisherman, and even Rory had hinted. Tass should have had more care to the sea, more care for his own life. The sea was a cruel mistress, as the old fisherman had said, and had given him no second chance. No respecter of age or inclination, she had seen her moment, and grabbed him for herself, forever.

As she slipped into sleep Rory's rugged countenance, sturdy frame, and dogged character somehow imposed itself upon the other image. With eyes half-closed to the wind, he stood like a rock by the wheel in her dreams, and rode the waves with respect for the might of the storm. He would not have allowed himself to acknowledge enjoyment until his boat lay moored within the confines of the harbour wall. Life, he believed, in his quiet way, was too precious to waste.

Stephanie awoke to a strangely quiet world. The storm had finally blown itself out. She wrapped herself in the duvet, went to the front door and stood for a while gazing out towards the bay. Though the air was bitter, it had been washed clean by the storm, and smelled fresh; and the clear view was lit by the alien glow of dawn.

A small flotilla of fishing boats came into view, chugged behind the sagging white cliff and were gone, leaving no more than a dark, fading wake behind them. In these days of over-fished waters and gloom and despondency, she was glad there were still men who fished. It reminded her of an old song: fishermen will always be, as long as fish swim in the sea.

Then just the lonely white sail of a keen sailor, risen early to catch the tide, lingered on the flat grey sea. Stephanie shivered, wondering if she would ever want to sail again. With the summer gone, it seemed a foolish thing to do.

Her mind, which should have been filled with the grief of Tass's untimely end, crept disobediently towards Rory's boatsheds, which were hidden from view. She wondered if he was out there working, or whether he still lay surrounded by sleep in the small, timbered room. She was very aware of him both as a compassionate human being, and as a man.

She allowed herself to muse on him fully, and to admit the attraction; and yet there was a very real fear that it was the result of circumstance. Was it because he had saved her life on the cliff that she now felt drawn to him? Was this what *rebound* meant? Needing someone so much that you latched onto the first person who was nice to you? The first person who treated you like a sensitive human, and not a cog in the working wheel.

Rory and Tass were polar opposites, despite their affinity with the sea. Where Tass had been slim, like steel cord wrapped in flesh, this man was thickset and sturdy. Where Tass had the easy white smile of a model, this man's smile came slowly from the depths of his being. Where Tass would stride into a fray with a battle light in his eye, Rory would stand back and think of an alternative. And yet he'd risked his life to save hers, and all those other people he rescued as he manned the lifeboat with other volunteers.

Tass had treated life as something to be grabbed with both fists, but Rory viewed it as a precious gift, to nurture, not squander.

She shivered, and went in, to sit in the draughty window-seat, her knees under her chin. Rory was not someone to toy lightly with. She told herself she'd be well advised to back off. Not that he had made any demands of her at all, in fact he'd been a perfect gentleman. Even the instant in the hut the previous evening, where she had been anticipating his kiss like a dewy-eyed teenager. Though, that might very well have been in her own imagination, instigated by a very real confusion over Tass's death.

They had made no arrangements for him to collect her today, and Stephanie decided that she should take her future into her own hands. She would see the people who had been close to Tass, then leave. She would tell him she was ready to go, and then do just that. He could make of it what he wanted. She had made her promise to him in a dazed state of mind, that was without doubt, but now she was going to manage her own future.

First and foremost, she wanted to talk to whoever had dived with Tass on that fateful day. From him she would learn exactly what had happened. Then she wanted to talk to Tass's uncle, the one who had been like a father to him and brought him up after his own father had walked away one day and never returned. What she would say to him, she wasn't quite sure, but it seemed discourteous, somehow, to come here, find out about Tass, and then leave without paying him a visit.

With these decisions firmly made, she dressed and was out of the cottage before eight O'clock, making her way down to the boatyard. The pickup was outside the shed, but of Rory there was no sign. A cold rising sun lit the puddles in the yard, accentuating the seedy and run-down state of the place. She hadn't paid much attention to it in the rain, but it was fairly obvious that little money had been spent there for rather a long time.

There was a sadness in seeing a place go to ruin, Stephanie couldn't help thinking. The once-thriving fishing community was on its last legs, and without it, maybe the boatyard was a dinosaur dying a slow death.

She wandered past the boat Rory was in

the process of repairing, and further along the side of the river estuary. It widened out to allow a few pleasure craft to moor, but many of them had already been lifted onto the hard-standing for the winter, leaving just the lonely orange buoys bobbing on the tide. Here and there a few craft remained, die-hards leaving the boats in for that possible winter sail, hoping that the early storms didn't tear them from the moorings and smash them into firewood.

Across the estuary the land flattened out into a wide swathe of waterbed overrun with rippling reed, above which the gulls still wheeled noisily.

Past the concrete platform with its raft of stranded, soiled yachts, and on a small path that tracked the estuary, Stephanie finally found Rory. He was bending over something in the verge.

He glanced up as she approached, and she saw that he was wrapping something up in his jumper. Something that was fighting and snapping at him. A brief acknowledgement lit his eyes.

'What is it?'

'A cormorant. It's got a punctured wing.'

Stephanie leaned closer, but by now the bird was well and truly smothered, its darting beak confined.

'How did that happen?'

Rory gathered it into his arms, and stood up, shrugging at the same time. 'I don't know. It looks as if it got caught up on something. A bit of metal, barbed wire? Whatever, I just had the devil of a job trapping it.'

His hand was laced with blood.

'You're bleeding!'

'It's not as bad as it looks.'

'We should clean it, anyway.'

'It's more important to get this to the vet, first. Damn thing's got a sharp beak!'

'Will the vet take it?' she asked dubiously.

He shook his head. 'He'll fix it, he's done it in the past, then I'll have to look after it until it can fly. There's a cage out the back.'

They made their way back to the sheds. 'It's a nice morning,' Rory commented companionably. 'It's always like this after a storm – tranquil and serene, as though the wind got worn out with yelling, and is taking a breather.'

'I saw a sailing boat out this morning, there must still be a bit of a breeze.'

'That'll be Jimmy. He's sailing his boat around to Exeter to moor it up for the winter. He likes to keep it in the water all year.'

'Isn't it a bit dangerous – I mean the storm and everything.'

Crows-feet snapped into place as he smiled.

'The storm's passed over. There's a new front coming, but he should get there before the weather closes in again.'

'I don't know much about the weather. I watch the forecast just to find out whether to take an umbrella to work'

'Not many people do. Unless your life depends upon it, you tend to see what's here rather than what's coming. A good sailor looks ahead. The sea is a dangerous playground.'

'Tass was experienced. He was with people who were experienced. I can't understand how he could die like that.'

Rory's lips narrowed. 'Accidents happen.'

'It's a dangerous sport, I suppose.'

'Like rock climbing, hang-gliding and caving. You just have to take care to minimise the possibility of accidents. Did you know more people are badly injured and even killed playing ball games than any of the so-called *dangerous* sports? It's a matter of statistics and perception. Aeroplanes are considered hazardous, but you don't think twice about driving a car, do you? Yet look at the numbers of people killed in car accidents; statistically it far outweighs those who get killed in plane crashes.'

'Yes, but with a crash, there are so many all at once, and they have no chance.'

'Each person who dies is an individual, not a statistic. If you dive, you can't get life insurance for love nor money, yet the chances of dying while diving are slim compared to the many other ways people discover to accidentally end their lives. You've got to take some chances, or life becomes stale. At least with sports it's possible to minimise the danger by planning; you can't do that when you climb on board a plane or get in a car – those accidents can be caused by someone else.' He would have said more, but clammed up. 'Get the keys to the truck, would you? They're on the table.'

'My car's here. I'll drive.'

'O.K. I'll hold the bird.'

Bending his head to fit his bulk awkwardly through the low door of her hatchback, he paused and asked, 'It's rather clean, are you sure you don't mind?'

Stephanie assessed Rory's working clothes and shrugged. 'Honest dirt, my father would have said.'

'Thanks.'

His tone was heavy with sarcasm, but he was smiling. She climbed in the driver's side. 'Where to?'

'Breminster. It's about eight miles, I'm

afraid. There's a veterinary surgery here, but it's only open twice a week.'

'All this for a bird?'

'Yes. Unless it was hurt really badly, then I'd wring its neck.'

She put the car into gear, casting a sidelong glance at Rory as she drove off. 'Could you?'

'I don't enjoy doing it, but I've done it before. I wouldn't leave it in pain.'

The storm had ripped much of the foliage from the trees, strewing it as debris along the lanes. Piles of sodden rust-brown leaves at the verges lent a seedy, exhausted appearance to the landscape; the exposed branches suggested winter had truly arrived.

Stephanie tried to concentrate on the driving rather than the man beside her who seemed to fill her car with his overwhelming presence. He smelled of some elusive aftershave or soap mingled with the varnish and wood-smoke impregnated into his clothes. Far from being repulsed, she found it strangely attractive.

She drove badly, changing gears awkwardly, and braking too hard. Rory didn't complain, but she caught the odd wince as the gears grated. Stoically he gave a steady stream of instructions until they arrived at an impressive eighteenth-century town-house onto the side of which the veterinary surgery had been added.

'Through the gate,' he said, and added out of sympathy for her inept driving, 'There's plenty of space to turn inside.'

'I'm in the wrong job,' she commented, peering up at the somewhat stately building.

'Maybe we all think that.'

'Do you? What would you do if you had the choice?'

'I think we'd best go in.'

The bird had remained quiescent in his arms for the whole drive, and now Stephanie looked at the muffled bundle as she parked. 'Is it still alive?'

'Most animals go quiet if they're covered,' he said. 'It'll show some fight in a moment, you'll see.'

He was right. The vet, a serious young man who called Rory *Mr Banner* at intervals, spread the wing while Rory kept the black beak at bay. She watched in amazement as he super-glued a flap of skin in place. She found it painful to watch, but the bird gave no more than a couple of annoyed cries.

When he'd finished, the vet looked up from washing his hands.

'That's the fifth stray waif you've brought me in the last year. I'd think you had enough problems without having to care for sick animals, too.'

Rory shrugged.

'It's no great deal.'

It was a gesture that Stephanie was beginning to recognise. It was not a dismissive gesture, but a token of acceptance. It meant he would do what he felt he had to do.

Was that what she was?

A stray that he'd picked up out of compassion?

'Can we leave it here for a couple of hours?'

The vet glanced around. 'I've got a spare cage. It's dopey at the moment, so I don't mind. I don't want it bashing itself to pieces in here, though, so not too long, eh?'

Rory took Stephanie's elbow.

'Come and have a look around Breminster. I'll buy you a coffee. Have you ever been here?'

'Thanks, and no I haven't.'

'There's not much to see, but the place has atmosphere. It was once a Victorian convalescing venue. People came here for sea bathing and fresh air, especially if they had TB, or consumption as they called it then.'

They left the car at the vets and walked up a long straggling hill into the small market town. There was an abundance of trees, and the houses were wide and squat, each surrounded by gardens, rather than the squashed-in, tall buildings in her home town.

'This is the posh end,' Rory explained. 'Quite a lot of retired folk come here, but at least most of the houses here are lived in by their owners.'

'There does seem to be a sort of friendly atmosphere.'

'In Townsea most of the large houses have been turned into hotels, and the small ones into holiday homes. In the summer, the place heaves, and in the winter, it dies. But you're right. This place still feels lived in during the winter.'

He sighed.

'In Townsea, though, there's a real problem in the winter. They lounge around in gangs and break windows because they have nowhere to go. That's why the hotels all get boarded up, making the place look like a war zone.'

'That's sad. Isn't there any work at all?'

'There are a few small businesses, but they're struggling. Nearly everything is geared around the holiday trade. Many kids up and run as soon as they're old enough, leaving the ones who haven't got the guts or brains to leave.'

'Like Tass?'

Rory frowned. 'Sorry, I forgot for a moment. But I didn't mean Tass. He was in a class of his own. He had plans, grand schemes. He would have gone, when the right opportunity presented itself. No, I meant the ones who wallow in unemployment and blame society, blame their parents, and blame everyone except themselves.'

'There are young people like that everywhere.'

'In a seaside town it's worse than anywhere else. In the summer there are arcades, clubs, leisure centres, sea sports. The teenagers associate with people in a holiday frame of mind, with lots of money to spend. But in the winter, it's dead. Everything is closed, boarded up. Things are vandalised, covered in graffiti, then the next summer it starts again. Some of our young people pull through and eventually find a niche in life, some drift out to the cities, but can't cope because they don't belong because they have no sense of place anymore.'

'You paint an incredibly distressing picture. Where did you fit in to all this as a youth?'

'I was a leaver out of choice. I looked at my home town, hated it, and escaped to the navy for a while.'

'But you came back.'

'Yes. I liked the work, but like all the Forces, conformity was hot on the agenda.'

'And you didn't conform?'

'Not easily. I came out on compassionate leave, because Dad was ill. But also, I was one of the 'lucky' ones because I inherited.'

'A run-down boatyard?'

He cast a quizzical glance.

'It makes me a landowner, a somebody. And my run-down boatyard has what they call Prime Location value. A large hotel chain has been trying to buy me out for a while.'

'Are you going to sell?'

'No.'

He didn't qualify the flat statement.

The long hill levelled, and the larger houses gave way to smaller town-houses, then to shops. It was more like an inner-city street than a holiday town. There were supermarkets and charity shops and men's outfitters.

'Is there anything you need?'

'I'd better get a few more groceries if I'm going to stay for a few days.'

'Are you?'

She looked at him seriously.

'This morning I absolutely wasn't, but now I don't know. I feel like a fraud, actually. I don't think I'm grieving for Tass, so much as grieving for a lost dream. I should go back to work, but I don't want to. I would be leaving unfinished business.'

She paused, and he waited for her to finish.

'I'm getting the sense that there's a mystery involved in Tass's death. He was so –' She searched for the right words. 'He was so *clever*, I just can't see him having some stupid accident, getting trapped. I want to talk to someone who dived with him that day.'

'I thought you would. I've arranged to meet Jimmy in the bar tonight. He can tell you.'

'Jimmy? The one who sailed out this morning?'

'Yes. He'll be into Exeter by early evening, and will get a lift back home. He's Tass's cousin.'

'Oh. I didn't know he had a cousin.'

'You didn't know much about him.'

It wasn't a derogatory statement, but fact.

'Tell me.'

They were approaching a small cafe, and Rory opened the door for her. They found a small round table covered in brightly patterned yellow oilcloth.

'Coffee or tea?'

'Coffee please. Americano with a touch of milk.'

Stephanie settled on a seat where she could watch the world go past while Rory got the coffee. He was so placid, so easy to be with, but he emanated the aura of a bear in hibernation, one that could come out fighting if needed. He had anger, strength and vitality, but just didn't wear them on his sleeve as Tass had.

He turned and caught Stephanie staring, and his gaze softened slightly in response as he walked towards her, the large cups dwarfed by his hands.

'I bought a couple of scones, too.'

'Thanks.'

He sat down, pushed a plate over to her, and they began to butter the scones as he talked.

'Tass's mother died in a car accident a year after he was born, and his father just walked away one day and didn't come back. Nobody knows why, or what happened to him, or even if he's still alive. Tass's uncle, Thomas, took him in and raised him. He didn't have a family of his own.

'There's a third brother, too, Martin Purdie, that's Jimmy's father. Both the brothers fish out of Townsea, as did Tass's father before he scarpered, but Tass wouldn't. He said he was meant for better things. He always thought that his father would one day turn up and take him away, having made a fortune in America, or something. It's more likely that he died destitute, because he had a drink problem before he even left, and he turned strange after Cathy, Tass's mother, died.'

'Poor, confused boy,' Stephanie said. 'To lose his mother and father, like that.'

'He was too young to remember them,' Rory said. 'But everyone was a bit soft on him for similar reasons. He was a charming boy, quick, intelligent – but even then, he used it to his advantage.'

'You're portraying someone rather selfish.'

'He was.' Rory grimaced. 'But people liked him, too, they couldn't help it. He had looks and something more: charisma. I liked him, too, in spite of what I've said. If only he had stopped hankering after that other life…'

He paused, then carried on.

'His father's boat was long sold, and he never stopped demanding the money from that sale, even though it had fed and clothed him since his father disappeared.'

'That must have hurt his uncle.'

'Thomas won't hear a word against him.' There was warning in the words. 'He was incredibly hurt by his younger brother's disappearance. He took Tass in, brought him up, loved him as his own son.' Rory sighed. 'It's in the past, now.'

Beyond the plate-glass, the street outside was waking up, finally. Approaching mid-morning, shoppers were beginning to emerge. But there was still a sleepy quality to the movements, not the frenzied and anxious scurrying that Stephanie was used to in the city.

'It's very peaceful here,' she said. 'It's hard to believe that terrible things are going on in the world when you sit and look at this.'

'Terrible things happen in small towns, too.'

She paused fractionally. 'I suppose they do.'

'You don't belong in the city, Stephanie,' Rory said. 'You're like that bird with a broken wing – wrapped in cloth, not struggling against fate because you can't see out. You belong in a place like Breminster, or Townsea - where you can sail and dive through the summer, and enjoy the solitude of winter.'

Stephanie was amused. 'What makes you think I wouldn't hanker after the night-life, the city, the shops?'

Unexpectedly he reached over and took one of her hands in his own. The shock of contact sent her pulse racing, and her eyes flying to his. Beneath the thatch of hair, his eyes were sincere. 'You've lived in both worlds. Where do you feel most content?'

'I don't belong here,' Stephanie said. 'I'm afraid I'd be like your teenagers, hankering after something a little livelier. I'm a blow-in, don't you recall, and will move on with the breeze.'

His hand withdrew. He shook his head.

'You said it yourself, that you didn't love Tass, you loved what he stood for: the wild and untameable, open air, freedom. You can still have that.'

Tears suddenly came to her eyes. 'It's such a waste! I still find it hard to believe he's just gone. One minute there, the next gone. I mean he touched me, made love to me, and now I – I feel sick.'

The scone sat like a lead balloon in her middle.

Rory stood hastily. 'Loo or fresh air?' he asked.

'Outside,' she whispered.

He grasped her elbow and the air hit her lungs, diminishing the sense of panic that had risen out of nowhere.

She found herself walking down a narrow, claustrophobic lane. There were tall houses one side, and a six-foot wall the other.

But the nausea was receding.

Then they stepped through an intricate wrought iron gate into sunshine. It was a small walled garden, perhaps once belonging to the large seafront houses that had been gutted to make shops. Still divided into small, formal flowerbeds edged by red bricks, the garden was a time-warp from the

Victorian era, including the moss-covered statue of a cherub patiently holding a bird-bath.

They walked the length of the garden in silence, her with her hand on Rory's arms, for all the world like a pair of Victorians taking the sea air.

It made her smile.

'What?' he asked.

'I feel like the grand lady, parading for my health.'

'All you need is a long skirt, some sunshine, a parasol and a paramour.'

'Paramour,' she echoed. 'What a delightful term. Is that someone courting, or an illicit lover?"

'I'm not sure. The word just popped into my head. We'll look it up when we get home.'

She reached into her bag for her mobile. Rory put his hand on hers, pushed it back. 'Don't break the moment. Leave technology where it belongs. At home.'

They ended up back at the gate.

'Are you feeling better? I wish I could do something to make it easier.'

'You are doing something. A lot. I'm sorry. I thought I had it under control.'

'I thought I did, too,' he muttered.

'I don't understand. You've known about it for months.'

He turned her to face him, put his hands on her shoulders. 'I'm not talking about Tass. I'm talking about the way I feel about you.'

She was taken aback, 'How you feel about me?'

He turned abruptly and they were walking side by side, not touching. His eyes were scanning the distance, and there was a slight flush to his cheeks.

'I, ah, wanted you from the moment I saw you in the summer. You didn't even see me, but I've been thinking of nothing else. I wanted to come and find you, but I wasn't sure how to do it. I don't mean I couldn't *find* you. I mean, I couldn't just turn up on your doorstep and say, now Tass is gone, do you *see* me.'

'If these are distracting techniques, they're not making me laugh.'

But he was serious, struggling to find words to express something that had been bottled up for a long time. And he was right, she hadn't seen him. She'd only had eyes for Tass.

'There was a time I could have murdered Tass, because he *used* you, and I wanted to know you. And when he died, I felt bad, as though I'd wished it upon him, somehow, and loathed myself for that thought.'

'Oh, goodness,' she said inadequately.

He smiled faintly. 'Yes, Oh, goodness.'

They walked in silence for a while, out onto the esplanade, a long path recently bounded by a curving sea wall. In the distance there was a small Victorian Pier, a cast iron affair with a jumble of buildings that probably housed ice-cream parlours and showed Victorian peep shows in the summer.

She was slightly stunned.

No, more than slightly.

All the while she'd been with Tass, Rory had been watching, wishing she'd been with him? And all the while she'd been at home dreaming of Tass, Rory had been dreaming of her?

It was bizarre.

But now he was talking again, looking out to sea as if afraid he'd see derision in her eyes, or worse, amusement.

'You didn't see me watching you. How should you? With Tass there to beguile and lie his way into your heart. But Tass knew.' The way he spoke the name was almost a curse. His voice softened. 'That's why he was so seductive toward you. He'd never kept a girl for more than a few days before. He called them holiday lays, but he knew how I felt about you, and was letting me know he could do what he wanted.'

Stephanie was stunned by his revelation.

'You think he went out with me to hurt *you*?'

'I don't think it, I know it. So now you'll hate me, and when I wake up tomorrow you'll be gone, and I'll berate myself for a fool, and be upset because I should have let you hold on to your dream.'

Before she could think of a response, he carried on in a low voice, not looking her way at all. 'When I saw you by the cliff I knew you'd found out about Tass. I parked the truck and ran all the way up the cliff path, and you were standing there, right on the edge, staring into the water. I shouted to you, but what with the rain and the wind – then you were gone. I thought you'd thrown yourself after him. And I knew he wasn't worth it.'

His eyes closed, and he winced with the memory. She reached for his hand, and he clutched it hard. Stephanie had moved into a strange place, a where revelations were not so much a shock, as someone pulling the curtain back on a past day, showing the truths she'd been too blind to see.

His revelations made her feel stupid.

She'd been older than Tass, infatuated, besotted like some stupid teenager, and Tass had been manipulating her feelings to be spiteful to *Rory*? Had she been aware of that at the time? She wanted to believe she had, but honesty made her realise she had just been euphorically happy. Drunk on the attention. Revelling in the fact that this glorious creature had been attracted to her.

And she'd been a holiday lay? 'Jesus. That's all a bit tawdry. It seems, there's none so blind as a girl in love.'

She stopped, turned to face the iron-grey sea and began to chuckle through her tears. She was furious, and embarrassed. She pulled her hand from Rory's and leaned forward onto the smooth white concrete wall.

He reached out, hesitantly. 'I didn't mean to upset you. It's just that, well, the truth hurts, but being ignorant is far more hurtful in the end. Especially if you're going to see Jimmy, or anyone.'

She stood and wiped her eyes. 'And they all knew, of course.'

His silence said it all.

After a while, she said, 'I'm glad you told me. I feel so stupid.'

'You shouldn't. Just remember how happy you were. I remember that. When you turned up you were pale and quiet, and when you left you were, oh, vibrant and alive. I was so jealous it hadn't been me that had caused it.'

'I'm having trouble taking all this in.'

'I'm sorry.'

She reached for his hand again as they strolled back to the car. She wasn't the only one who was finding it hard.

So, this was why Rory had asked her to stay.

Not so much to get over Tass's death, but to learn the truth behind her romance, which hadn't been a romance at all. It was a revelation that had come at her sideways. She hadn't been expecting it. And the more she thought about those short weeks in the summer, the more she remembered Rory as a quiet adult presence behind the small knot of Tass's mates. He'd been there, driving the dive boat. He'd been there in the pub in the evenings, he'd been there, sitting on the sea wall as they'd swum from the beach. They'd gone out in his sailing boat.

And she had been thinking of him as some kind of mentor. An adult presence to make sure the kids were OK. He'd been a silent presence, almost not there at all. And Tass had been playing with her affections to hurt him. 'Why would Tass have wanted to hurt you like that,' she asked finally.

'Because he was jealous. I owned the boatyard, and he owned nothing but his dreams. He thought the fates had something against him, because he didn't own all the stuff he saw around. He wished he owned the hotel, the boatyard, a house, anything. He so much wanted to be *someone*.'

'He was someone.'

'All he could see was what he didn't have. I felt sorry for him, when I wasn't being angry. He was his own worst enemy. With his character, he would have made his way, sooner or later. But he didn't want to wait. He wanted everything *now*.'

'You're portraying a very bitter person.'

'Behind all that gung-ho stuff, and his outward persona, he *was* bitter. It was a canker that killed him in the end.'

They had reached the turning into the vet's drive. Stephanie stopped and pulled Rory to face her. 'Rory, hold me. Just for a moment.'

He wrapped his arms around her tightly. He was so broad, so strong, she was enveloped in his embrace. Her face was pressed into his shoulder; his chin rested briefly on top of her head.

When she pulled away he stepped back quickly, as if worried she might think he was taking advantage.

'When you saved my life up on the cliff,' she said, 'I wasn't trying to kill myself. I told you that.'

'You did.'

'What I meant was, life is too precious. I wouldn't have done that for any man. Not

Tass. Not you.'

'I'm pleased to hear it.'

There was no sarcasm in his voice. She looked up and their eyes locked. For the second time, she sensed that he was going to kiss her. She didn't turn away, but the kiss he fleetingly planted on to her lips left her feeling betrayed. She wanted more.

Rory laughed bitterly at himself. 'You're right when you said I hardly know you. I've been mooning like a teenager in heat, and maybe it's all just jealousy after all. Or anger, because Tass was laughing at me. You'd better see Jimmy tonight, and then leave before I become a right pain.'

He marched towards the vet's surgery. Stephanie had to scuttle to catch up.

They collected the injured cormorant, and the drive back seemed shorter than the drive out.

At the boatyard, Rory climbed out, carefully nursing the bird. He didn't ask her to stop or come in. She realised he needed solitude to ponder on what had been said, and whether it should have been said at all. She needed time to digest the information, too. But one thing she didn't doubts, was that he was telling the truth.

'I'll pick you up at six,' he said, over his shoulder. 'We're meeting in the hotel. We can have a meal before Jimmy arrives.'

'Oh, yes. I forgot. Thank you.'

He gave sardonic grimace, and she knew he was thinking: thank me, for what? She looked in the mirror as she drove away. He was standing there staring after her, the cormorant hugged in his arms.

She stopped at the garage and bought some essentials and a book before returning to the cottage, but somehow her mind was filled with so many things she found herself reading the same pages over and over, not making any sense of them.

Rory wanted her. She could see it in every line of his body, every nuance of movement. Tass had known, and had taunted him with her, and she hadn't realised?

She felt like a fool. She had been a fool.

Rory's sexuality had filled the small car on the way home, lighting fires she had thought would never be lit again. What she hadn't been able to work out was *why* she felt that way.

How could she come here two days ago believing herself wildly in love with Tass, and transfer that need straight to Rory? It wasn't right, it wasn't natural. She burst into tears, but this time it had nothing to do with Tass's death.

Chapter 5

When Jimmy Purdie came into the bar, Stephanie didn't need to be told. She'd never seen him before, but he stopped inside the door and stared at her across the room with Tass's sultry eyes. He was of a similar build, too. The same lean figure Tass had been so proud of, the same clean-cut features, slightly narrowed. It was hard to pinpoint it, but where Tass had charisma, his cousin did not.

Recognising Rory, Jimmy wove his way through the tables and joined them, dropping his wet-weather gear from his shoulders as he came.

'Sit,' Rory said, indicating. 'I'll get a drink. This is Stephanie, by the way.'

'I remember.'

But whatever he remembered, Jimmy held out his hand formally, and Stephanie took it, feeling strangely moved by the gesture. Tass would never have done that, and it served to distance the two men in her mind. With the same soft west-country accent his voice was similar, but lower than Tass's. He also seemed more mature; though, surely, he was the younger?

As if realising she was making a mental comparison, Jimmy said, 'People often thought we were brothers.'

She nodded. 'You could be.'

'I'm sorry we didn't contact you. We didn't know we should. Tass had a lot of friends, one way or another.'

Stephanie no longer felt hurt by that revelation. She didn't know if the past tense referred to Tass or the girls he had dated, and gave a rueful smile.

'So I understand. I wasn't the first, or even the last, so why should you think I was any different?'

He stared at his hands. 'I don't really want to talk about it, but Rory told me what happened up on the cliff. I wouldn't want Tass to be the cause of your death.'

'It was an accident. I was being careless. Rory saved my life, even while thinking I didn't want it saved, and now he's trying to be my counsellor as well.'

When Jimmy smiled, it was genuine, lighting his whole, tired face. 'He would. He wants to sort out everybody's problems except his own. And with these grand schemes of his, he's doing his best to alienate even those who like him.'

'What grand schemes?'

'Oh, trying to bring new life into the town, with a project the locals are dead set on fighting. He's rowing against the tide, but I think he knows that.'

'He didn't tell me anything about it. I've only been here a short while, and I've probably bored him to tears with talk of Tass.'

She flushed.

'I didn't mean it to sound that crass. You must be still mourning.'

'We're here to talk about Tass, not me,' Rory butted in, placing three pints on the table.

'Perhaps we should be talking about you, though,' Jimmy said seriously. 'You're always trying to do things for other people. Perhaps you should think of yourself, for a change.'

'What I do is my business, in the end.'

It was said with finality.

'Then you have to accept the consequences. You can't have it all ways.'

Jimmy downed half the pint in one go, and leaned back with a sigh.

'Good trip?' Rory asked.

'Passable.' He flexed stiff shoulders. 'Would you believe the wind died on me and I had to motor the last few miles?'

'Highly galling,' Rory said, his smile belying the sarcasm in his voice.

He glanced at Stephanie. 'These die-hard sailors feel cheated when they have to use the engine. That's what it's there for.'

'Don't listen to him,' Jimmy told her. 'He's a rag- -and-pole merchant himself on the quiet. The tatty blue bilge-keeler alongside the shed is his baby.'

'I know, we went out in it in the summer,' she admitted. 'I like to sail a bit, myself. When I get the chance. Working full time in the city drains incentive.'

'If that's your passion, you should move nearer to the water. You only get one chance at this life, it's a shame to let your job rule it,' Jimmy said.

'That's what I told her.'

There was friendship here, Stephanie realised, a friendship deep enough for Rory to ask this youth to talk about his loss to a stranger. At that moment she didn't want to have to ask him about Tass, he seemed so content.

But even as these thoughts crossed her mind, Jimmy pushed his hair out of his eyes, and said to her, 'So, what do you know?'

'I heard he dived off the Mary Jane, went into one of the cabins, and a beam fell, cutting his airline, and blocking the entrance at the same time. That's all.'

Jimmy nodded.

'That's about it. We'd actually gone down with some cutting equipment earlier because there were a few areas we were going to make safe. It had been planned for ages.'

'The wreck is just under forty feet at high tide, as you know, so we just had forty minutes with a short decom. We'd planned to do it in two dives, with a full 24 hours between. You know the old maxim, plan the dive, and dive the plan? Well, Tass was arguing to just go and finish the job, but we wouldn't. so, he took it into his own hands. We only realised he'd gone back out when someone noticed the rib wasn't at the moorings. When we saw the keys were gone, we realised it could only have been Tass.'

'Why would he do that?

'That's what Tass was like. He'd worked out the decompression times, and thought he could just go and get it finished, and still be within the safety margin.'

'Who found him?' Stephanie questioned softly, almost hesitantly.

'I did. We had to scrabble round to find a boat to borrow, find lifting gear, and get our tanks charged. He'd been dead a while by the time we got out there. It took three of us and some tackle to move the beam enough to get his body up. We had several boats out helping, by then. Everyone knew it was a recovery.'

'I can't believe he'd put himself in that kind of danger.'

'No. He shouldn't have been there on his own.'

Jimmy looked down into his beer. 'The beam was already unsound, and we'd made it worse, getting the job half-done, but we were going to finish it the next day. Quite a few people dive there, so we left a notice on the wreck-buoy that no-one should dive it until we'd made it safe. We'd done it all by the book. We thought we'd forestalled the possibility of an accident, then he went back out on his own. I should have known he would.'

There was self-derision in his voice. 'We'd freed one side, and the plan was to prop it while we cut the bolts at the other end, then hang the beam on buoyancy bags, and pull the props when we were clear. From what we could gather, he'd cut one of the bolts, but before he could get to the other, it snapped under the strain.'

'I don't get it. Why would he do that? Tass was a bit gung-ho, but he wasn't stupid.'

He shrugged. 'Tass always knew best. He lived in a different world to the rest of us. It all came out in the enquiry. There were four of us there to verify what had happened, and there was a verdict of accidental death. No-one was blamed.'

Jimmy said it almost harshly as if expecting her to question his word. He hadn't had to add the last sentence. It was almost an admission of guilt; complicity. As if the four divers who had recovered his body had solidified their story before reaching land. But if they had done that, they had something to hide. She couldn't imagine what. Unless Tass's death hadn't been an accident.

That would make it murder.

She shook the thought from her head. 'I'm sorry. I know it must be painful for you to talk about it.'

Jimmy grimaced. 'I'm told it gets easier with time. It's not something you have to face every day. I've never seen a dead body before, let alone someone I knew. I'd never recovered one before, and don't ever want to again.'

'No. I've never had to face a death that wasn't anticipated. Tass's death must have been a shock; especially as he was so young, and like a brother to you.'

'I said we looked like brothers,' Jimmy said, a hard light in his eye.

She was slightly shocked. Tass's own cousin had grown up with him, worked with him, dived with him, gone to the pub with him; but hadn't liked him? No, it was deeper than that, she realised.

He'd hated him. Could such hatred have led to murder? How easy to have done that in a place where a man had no chance to survive. She hid her appalled musings behind a drink.

Rory leapt into the gap and asked, 'How's Thomas these days?'

'Older.'

The tone of understated dislike transformed into sadness. 'Tass's death got to him big time. I don't think he'll ever go out on the trawler again.'

'Time will cure it. Fishing's in his blood.'

'He hasn't got that much time,' Jimmy said dryly. 'And there are things in a man's blood that you never guess until it comes to a crunch.'

Stephanie didn't think the embittered words referred to Thomas Purdie.

Rory seemed to miss the undercurrent. 'How's your Dad these days?'

There was that shrug again. 'Getting used to the idea. It was a shock to all of us.' He shook his head, then gave Stephanie a sardonic smile. 'Well, now you know. I don't really know why you came. You'll be moving on, tomorrow?'

Even in the dimmed light of the bar it was evident that he wanted her to go away and never come back.

Just then, a young woman, wrapped up heavily in coat and scarf slipped in behind Jimmy, put her hand on his shoulder. He glanced up.

'Janet. You ready to go on home, love?'

She nodded, then gave a sidelong, venomous glance at Stephanie. 'You should leave. You're not welcome here. You're not one of us. You don't know anything.'

'Hush,' Jimmy said, putting his hand on hers. 'There are things people need to come to terms with.'

She gave a snort of derision.

Stephanie realised more than anything that she was an outsider, a stranger to this tight-knit group. 'You're right, I should go. I'm making you all go over things you'd rather let lie. It's not my business, I guess.'

'No, it's not.' Now Jimmy was backing up Janet. 'Rory shouldn't have told you to stay.'

There it was again, that shut door, that cold shoulder. She didn't belong, and he was making it plain.

Jimmy rose and began to shrug himself into his waterproof. 'Is there anything else you want to ask?'

'Come on,' Janet insisted.

Stephanie flinched fractionally at the antipathy the girl wasn't remotely trying to hide. Why had Jimmy agreed to meet her when his girlfriend was so antagonistic? She had the feeling that there was a pact of secrecy, that he'd agreed to meet her to put her mind at rest and send her packing so that she didn't talk to anyone else. She shook her head denying his question and her stray thoughts at the same time.

'I'm sorry if this has caused pain,' she said hesitantly. 'It wasn't my intention.'

Jimmy had put his arm around Janet, and taken a step towards the door. He looked back. 'I know it wasn't,' he said candidly. 'I think you're probably a nice person. But we've all faced things in our dreams that we never thought to face in reality. If I was rude, I'm sorry. Rory, see you later. Janet needs to go home.'

He patted Rory on the shoulder and left without another word.

Rory stared into his empty glass as if he didn't want to look at her, Stephanie realised. He hadn't missed the undercurrents, after all, and was waiting for her to voice them.

He was waiting to lie to her.

The morning's empathy died. Rory was one

of *them* and she was an outsider. Something had happened out there under the water, and he knew about it. She sensed his frustration. He'd been trying to palm her off with Jimmy's honest testimony, but it had backfired. If he hadn't arranged the meeting with Jimmy, she would have been none the wiser.

'I want to speak to Thomas,' she said bluntly.

'No.' Rory's tone was adamant.

'You can't stop me.'

He added a plea. 'Thomas won't want your condolences, and you'll do nothing but harm – he's been through enough.'

'You should've thought of that when you asked me to stay.'

'I wasn't thinking straight.' He toyed with the empty glass and added softly. 'Jimmy was right. I should have sent you home straight away.'

'Why? So I didn't get involved?'

His mouth pursed. 'Involved in what?'

'That's what I'd like to know.'

'Now you're being melodramatic. Tass is dead. There was a diving accident. Just accept the facts. Come to terms with it, that's all I wanted you to do, not start inventing things that didn't happen.' Rory shifted uncomfortably in his seat. 'Do you want another drink, or shall I take you home?'

'Home?'

He flushed faintly. 'To the cottage.'

'Oh,' her ingenuous wonder made him scowl. 'To *your* home, you mean.'

Rory slammed his glass down and stood up. 'I think we've done enough soul searching for one day.'

He walked beside her to where the truck was parked, and opened the passenger door with quick, brittle movements before walking around to the other side, and even that small courtesy fired her irritation. But he didn't drive on up the hill, he turned down, towards the boatyard.

'What are you doing?'

'We need to talk. I was always told not to go to bed on an argument.'

'We haven't argued.'

'Your anger is like a brick wall between us. You feel betrayed, you think you know what happened out there. You think I'm part of it.'

He pulled into the boatyard and cut the engine.

'I'm past talking, tonight. Would you please just take me back up to the cottage. I need to be alone.'

'Please, I just –'

She climbed down, slammed the door, and slung her bag over her shoulder. 'If you won't take me, I'll walk.'

Rory leapt out, half ran around the truck and blocked her path. Intensely aware of his size and strength, and the fact that she barely knew him, she backed a step, her eyes widening.

Rory winced, and held his hands out in a defensive manner. 'I'm sorry. I didn't mean to scare you. You know I wouldn't hurt you. It's just that I can't let you go away thinking that Jimmy's a murderer. He's not.'

'Take me back up to the cottage, please?'

He walked to the driver's door, defeated.

'I'm sorry I scared you. Believe me, I didn't mean to do that.'

Stephanie hesitated for no more than a second.

'O.K. I'll listen to you, but it'd better be good.'

Inside *the hut*, as he called it, Rory turned on the lights and opened the Rayburn. As the heat blasted out, he opened a can and thrust it at her.

She took it automatically, her fingers brushing against his in passing.

She blanched involuntarily.

Rory swore under his breath, and backed off to stand against the Rayburn's rail. He took a deep breath. 'Jimmy wouldn't want me to tell you this. He thought he could tell

123

you the facts and you'd just go away, but you're too quick. You pick up on the subtext. He and Tass weren't close. In fact, something had happened between them that led to a fight.' Her breath caught. 'Obviously, when Tass died, peopled wondered... and one of the first questions that was asked was who stood to gain.'

'I thought he didn't own anything?'

'No, but he stood to inherit. Both Thomas's and Martin's cottages are owned by them, and the two boys were each the sole beneficiary of one cottage, and the beneficiary by default of the other if one of them died. So, Jimmy stood to inherit both.'

'Tass was murdered for financial gain?'

'No! I didn't say that. But people began to whisper, wondering whether Jimmy was capable of killing Tass. Rumours spread like viruses. These old fishermen's cottages might seem insignificant, but they're fetching a high price today.'

'But you're talking maybe years into the future, unless Thomas is ill.'

'One murder, two, three? Where does it stop? And if you were clever, who would know? A diving accident for a diver, a heart attack for an old man...' Stephanie sat up straighter, and Rory laughed without humour. 'I said rumours started. I didn't say he did it. Jimmy's incapable of killing in cold blood like that. Could you? You know what it's like down there. Could you cut off another man's escape to the surface and stand by while he drowned? Could you?'

She found herself shaking her head as his voice rose passionately.

'Well neither could Jimmy. Just take my word for that. Those weeks during the autopsy and the inquest were hell for Jimmy. The papers had a field day, and the whole town was divided into those who thought he did and those who believed he didn't, long before the verdict.' He grimaced. 'There are still those who don't believe the verdict. Shit sticks, don't forget.'

'So, he didn't do it? It was really an accident?'

'Are you prepared to believe me and the result of the enquiry, or are you going to make your own decision, too?'

There was challenge in the words, but Stephanie remembered the desperation in the depths of Jimmy's eyes and understood the stress under which such accusation must have placed him.

'My honest gut reaction? Jimmy's a good bloke. I don't believe he killed Tass.'

Rory ran his hand through his hair again, tiredly. 'You're not mourning Tass anymore, there's no great mystery to solve, and I assume you'll you be leaving tomorrow.'

It was as if she had been dismissed. 'I'm free to go?'

'You were always free to go.'

They weren't the words she wanted to hear, somehow. 'I still feel that I ought to speak to Tass's uncle.'

Rory sighed. 'You're like a dog with a bone. But if you must, you must. I'll take you. But I warn you now, you won't be welcome.'

'Then why would you do that when you don't want me to go there in the first place?'

'I don't know. I keep trying to stop myself from interfering. There are times I could just walk away from this bloody soap opera I seem to be living in and never come back.'

'You said that before.'

'Yes, but I won't. When you said I loved the place, you were right, but it's a sort of love-hate relationship. Sometimes I feel I'm a prisoner here.'

'Trapped by conscience?'

'And narrow-mind traditions. And loneliness.' He wiped a hand over his eyes. 'I don't want to be alone right now. My honest and annoyingly determined Stephanie, will you walk with me, along the shore?'

Where else.

He stood hunched by the door, hands in the pockets of his once-waterproof sailing jacket, watching as she zipped up hers. Then, as she approached, he withdrew a hand and held it out to her; she put her own into it, not knowing if they were friends soon to become lovers, or strangers about to part.

The wind had dropped, the clouds lifted, the night sky speckled with stars. Coloured lights from the esplanade wove in eerie reflection in the dark water. The soft surge of waves and the ever-present grinding of pebbles in the undertow filled the night, encompassing their loneliness.

At Rory's side, her hand still in his, Stephanie experienced a deep sense of contentment, never experienced before. It was as if he'd reached out not just his hand, but his very essence, to wrap her and keep her warm.

As if sensing her thoughts, Rory's hand tightened fractionally. 'Look at her now. The sea, I mean. It hardly seems possible that only yesterday she was ripping the buoys from their chains and reaching over the breakwater with enough fury to crack the foundations,' he said, finally.

'Why do men think the sea is female?'

There was a flash of white teeth. 'Enormous tantrums, beauty and serenity, mingled with the voice of seduction. What else should she be, but a woman?'

Stephanie smiled. She pulled her hand from his, bent to reach a stone, and threw it out into the dark water. The esplanade lights disintegrated into a cascade of glass fragments, then slowly melded again. Conscious that Rory was still watching her, her movements became clumsy and embarrassed.

'Don't run away,' he said.

Stephanie gave a flustered laugh at the depth of emotion in his voice. 'A few moments ago, it seemed as if you were trying to make me leave.'

'I was scared of what would happen if you stayed. I was scared of the dream turning sour. I still am.'

She stopped short, frowning, about to argue, but Rory reached out, and gently turned her face towards him. Even while common sense urged her not to do so, her face even lifted slightly towards his as he bent his head to kiss her.

This was no fleeting peck on the lips as before, but a tentative question all the same. One to which Stephanie should have answered with rejection, but it was beyond her. She wanted his touch with a need quite out of proportion to rational thought.

Where his lips touched her with diffident question, hers knew no such hesitation. Almost delirious with the cold, the trauma, and the alcohol, she buried her small niggle of doubt in some dark recess, responding with all the release of pent-up frustration.

Feeling the unhesitating urgency of her response, Rory needed no second invitation. She found herself engulfed in an embrace that crushed her against his oilskins. Their kiss was almost shocking in its intensity. Astounded by the almost tangible force which leapt between them, Stephanie's eyes flew open, searching for comprehension; but the night was dark, the kiss long, and Rory's arms a haven in an insecure world.

Gradually the sullen sea intruded and clashed with the peace in her mind. She shivered, sensing Tass's ghostly form watching, a smile on its lips: see, you're no better than me. The unspoken words mingled with the pebbles agitated by the fingers of salt water.

It took Rory a moment to realise that she was no longer responding, that she was pushing against him. He released her reluctantly, his own breath shortened with obvious desire.

'I need to go back,' she demanded, close to tears. 'Take me back to the cottage, please.'

Rory pushed his hand through his hair. 'I'm sorry,' he apologised, 'I didn't intend for that to happen.'

He stood there like some confused shaggy dog that had been reprimanded, and Stephanie felt her heart reach out. 'It's too soon,' she said. 'It's just too soon.'

Rory's face softened. 'Of course it's too soon. I should have known. Come on,' he said. 'I'll drive you up to the cottage.'

They walked together in silence.

Several times Stephanie sensed that Rory was about to speak, but each time she felt the faint withdrawal before he did so. When he did speak, she knew it was not what he'd been intending to say. 'I don't want you to leave, Stephanie.' He rolled her name from his tongue like a lover's caress. 'I want you to stay here, with me.'

'But?'

Air whistled through his teeth in perplexity.

'I'm torn. When I said I wanted to help you come to terms with Tass's death, I meant it. But it was a selfish request, too, because I wanted to see if you could learn to like me. I didn't think of it stirring everything up. Your being here is hurting too many people.'

They had reached the lane where the pick-up waited. In the glare of a security light,

Rory opened the doors, and Stephanie could see the harrowed expression on his face as she clambered in.

'Jimmy was right, Rory,' she said. 'You want to sort out everyone else's problems. Tell me honestly, do *you* want me to leave tomorrow?'

There was a hesitant pause, partially covered as he fumbled with the key and started the vehicle, then he answered in little more than a hoarse whisper. 'No. I don't want you to leave.'

'Then I shan't,' she said. 'And you have to accept some people might not like it. But I'll make no more promises. I can't be with you unless I'm certain.'

'You mean about the way Tass died?'

'No, about you. Trust requires honesty, and you're not being honest.'

He slumped a bit further into the seat. 'Tass's death opened a real can of worms, but it really was an accident. There are just too many people who have already been hurt. It's not my place to interfere.'

'You mean you've made some sort of promise to keep hidden whatever it is you're hiding. You feel honour bound to keep that promise even to the extent that you'd let me go, and never see me again?'

Once again, his silence was answer enough,

and she was silent, too, thinking of the implications.

'Is that a black point against me?' Rory said, eventually, trying to joke as he steered the cumbersome vehicle through the dark country lane.

'Being loyal? How can it be?' Stephanie said, a faint smile lifting the disturbed frown. 'It just means I have to work it out for myself. There's a kind of nobility in keeping mum for the sake of a promise, but maybe also stupidity. Like men duelling in the old days, standing heroically still to allow your opponent to take a pot shot. Fighting it out I could understand, but not that.'

'Well, of course not, you're a woman.'

'Thanks.'

He grinned at her, but there was more in his eyes than humour, and the tension lifted slightly.

When they reached the cottage, Rory didn't stop the motor. 'I won't embarrass us both by inviting myself in,' he said.

Stephanie leaned over and gave him a peck on the cheek, and his response was as brief. However, there was a faintly wicked look in her eye as she slid out, saying, 'My will-power suffered a serious knock tonight, too, so it's just as well you're going.'

Chapter 6

Contrary to her expectations, Stephanie slept better than she had the previous few nights. Somehow her very immediate and unexpected affinity with Rory was a balm to her confusion. He would always be a pillar of support to the woman in his life. His woman wouldn't lie awake at night wondering whether he'd be there for her the next day, she would simply know he would be.

On reflection, the next morning, what frightened her most was not whether he'd be there for *her*, but whether she could be there for him. Somehow, the fact that he'd been wanting her for months while she hadn't known of his existence was like discovering you'd been stalked.

It didn't make her comfortable.

Her first fear, that she was attracted to him on the rebound now seemed silly in the face of acceptance that Tass had been a ship passing in her night. Or she, his.

No, the harsh warning bell was that this

new attraction was too simple, too filled with possibilities, and too soon.

It had to end in disaster.

She lay drowsing in the morning warmth of her bed half wishing he was there in reality, half wondering when the bubble would burst, when she would land heavily back to earth with a painful thump.

Perhaps when she saw Rory again she would just see a weathered young man who was torn between two worlds. Perhaps there would be no quickening of the pulse, no flash of inner warmth as his heavy-lidded eyes raked her body and came back to dwell on her face.

Until she contemplated this, she hadn't remembered that he did just that, as if he was just making sure her body was as he remembered, before looking up to her features for harmony of thought.

Another fear was, he wasn't as strong as he seemed at first glance. He was vulnerable. She could hurt him very easily. Only once before, he told her, had he allowed his feelings to develop for someone, only to end up betrayed by that love. She didn't want to be the second.

He'd made it clear that he was more than a little bit interested in her, but she knew he wasn't seeking some brief romance. He would want it to be forever, with all the strings of commitment, children, old age. If they embarked on a serious relationship and she changed her mind, Rory would be badly hurt.

She was standing on the edge of a whirlpool of emotion, and it would take just one false step to be sucked into something she couldn't climb out of, and she'd been horribly independent all her life.

Since the age of sixteen she'd taken her future into her own hands, allowing no-one to talk her into becoming something she didn't want to be. In spite of good grades, she'd had no wish to go to University, though her parents tried hard to persuade her. She chose, instead, to take a two-year secretarial course, then make her way out into the world.

'But what about a career, darling?' her mother had persuaded. 'You don't want to end up as someone else's servant for the rest of your life, and that's what a secretary is!'

'I don't want to be a career girl,' she'd replied placidly. 'I want a job, a family, then one day a job again in that order. I don't want to end up being torn between a career and a home. I don't want to be some high-flying solicitor or marketing director, hiding my ulcers behind some glossy lipstick and designer suits.'

Stephanie had been upset that there had been no talk of happiness, no talk of what she would like out of life.

They had wanted the best for her but hadn't seen beyond their own foiled dreams.

And it seemed Rory was offering everything she'd argued for; added to which, he owned a very nice cottage. She gazed around the bedroom. Yes, it was comfortable, she could be happy here. As long as he put in central heating. He also owned real estate that could be sold to a big hotel chain, probably for a reasonable sum.

Her mother would probably think she'd done very well for herself. It was hard to separate the emotional from the financial, and what if she wasn't being honest to herself, never mind Rory? Would she really allow herself to be seduced by the thought of a comfortable life? One in which she didn't have to go back to a dead-end job with a boss she didn't like?

Her working life, despite deciding not to go for broke, hadn't been stress-free. Her comfortable little first job in a failing firm, from which she had been reluctantly made redundant after two years, had been the happiest of all of them.

The next job, her first real secretarial role,

she had quit because of her boss's arrogant manner, and the job she had now held was just as bad. She went in, did her work, and came home with a pay cheque, too tired to think of her next move.

Her mother hadn't actually said, *I told you so*, but the implication had been clear. Some jobs were successful, some less so, but she now realised her limitations weren't in lack of intellect, but in not being able to prove it. It seemed, the glass ceiling she had reached was one she had made for herself.

There had also been a few dates, mostly from the office, and most of whom had disappeared in a huff after not being invited in to coffee after a single night out. It seemed that being a secretary was like having a neon light on her head: bimbo up for some fun. Not one of these had been introduced to her Mum, much to her increasing disappointment.

She'd lost her virginity in a mild attack of calf-love at eighteen, which had seemed like the real thing for all of two weeks; but since then she'd wondered if she was destined never to meet anyone who simply *liked* her rather than wanting to have sex with her.

Tass had been an anomaly.

She tried to self-justify her actions, but decided that Tass had just been Tass, and who could have resisted him? Maybe he had just been born with an unfair dose of pheromones.

Her defences had been stormed without words – a look, a gesture, and she'd fallen for him as, in all likelihood, had all the other girls he seemed to have been with. Maybe they'd known the score. She'd been stupidly innocent, considering her age. Her mistake had been in not hiding her reaction to his magnetic appeal, and once seen, he'd taken advantage. It was easy to look back in hindsight and say it wouldn't happen again; that once stung, she'd have more savvy, but she'd been defenceless under the onslaught of his charisma.

He had confused her for the whole two weeks, and she still didn't know how it had happened. She'd been wounded by his casual attitude, at the same time as allowing herself to be seduced by his curved smile, his stunning eyes, and that innate magnetism he exuded.

She admitted now, this wounding had been self-inflicted and deliberate. Maybe, in her heart she'd known him for what he was. She had loved the experience and hated herself for going to him so easily. She had hated him for taking her so casually, but with more passion than she had ever experienced.

Never before had she ever been so alive. It was as if he had truly woken her out of a long, enchanted sleep, but one without the happily ever after. When she'd left, he'd promised to call, but had probably moved straight on to the next girl, blithely unaware or uncaring about the trail of unhappiness he left in his wake.

Rory was so very different. Where Tass had been careless in his appropriation of anything he wanted, Rory was reticent to take that which was not given with wholehearted reciprocation. She thought he would neither casually take love and discard it, nor give it lightly, which was why Stephanie knew she had to tread softly around the whirlpool – it wasn't just her future, but his too.

The sound of a telephone knocked her out of her reverie. She let it ring for a moment, then found herself bounding downstairs to answer it.

She hesitated for just a second, before saying, 'Hello?'

There was a pause, then a man's voice.

'Have I got a wrong number? I was looking for Rory.'

'This is Rory Banner's house.'

'Oh, right. Is he around?'

'No, he's at the boatyard. Have you got his

mobile number?'

'I've got it somewhere, but he's not very good at answering it.'

'I could take a message.'

'Great. It's pretty urgent. Tell him James Mayhew-Jones called from the Eco-Development Corporation. I'd like to meet up at one O'clock, today at the Mistletoe House Hotel. Sorry about the short notice, but can someone let me know if he can make it?'

'Of course. I assume he's got your number?

'I'll give it to you again just in case. And if he's wondering why the haste, tell him it's Thunderbirds are Go.'

Stephanie smiled. 'I haven't a clue what that means, but I'll tell him.'

'Whatever happened to your education? Oh, and he's welcome to bring a guest if you want to come too. It might do his image some good.'

'I'll mention that you said so.'

There was a chuckle as the man rang off.

Stephanie climbed back upstairs, and showered. When she was dressed, the phone went again.

This time it was Rory.

'Are you up and about?

'Pretty much.'

'Well, bacon's on the stove. Are you coming down for breakfast?'

'Give me fifteen minutes.'

The brief answer didn't convey the warmth generated in her breast at the sound of his slow voice. So, it hadn't worn off overnight. For some reason she whistled to herself as she drove seaward, and it had little to do with the sun that was trying to creep out from behind the clouds banking up against the cliffs.

She knocked briefly before opening the door.

Rory looked up from the pan, a deep smile of welcome creasing his whole face.

'Make yourself at home. Did you sleep well? Not worrying about things?'

'I seem to be able to do both at once.'

He laughed. 'Me, too.'

Perching her chin on her hands Stephanie watched as he deftly turned the browned bacon out onto hot plates.

'A man called James Mayhew-Jones phoned you this morning.'

'Oh?'

Rory carried the plates of bacon, eggs, and thick buttered slices of fresh bread to the small pine table.

'He wants to have lunch with you at one. At the, ah, Mistletoe House Hotel?'

'That's short notice. It's also in Plymouth, which is a bit of a drive. Did he say anything else?'

'He said tell you Thunderbirds are Go.'

He stilled for a moment. 'Well, now. Good.'

'He said I should come, too; it would do your image good.' His brows rose. 'I think he assumed, because I answered your phone early in the morning –'

'Does that bother you?'

'I'm not sure.'

'I'll make sure he knows you're a guest and I'm staying down here. Oh, we could say you're my secretary. He told me to get one, only I never got around to it.'

She laughed.

'But, actually, I could do with a secretary. Didn't you say that's what you do? In all honesty, I really am the most unorganised person when it comes to paperwork.'

'Are you joking?'

'No. I can't write a letter to save my life, and as for computers, well, I've seen 'em around, but never felt the attraction. Do you like your job?'

'Not at all.'

'Then think about it. This is an honest offer with no strings attached. And you'll be living by the sea and can go sailing whenever you want. Weather permitting, of course. Whatever you're getting paid I'll equal it and throw in accommodation.'

She was gobsmacked.

'But – I thought you were broke?'

'I don't think I ever actually said that. You don't have to answer right away. Eat your breakfast.' He gave a fleeting grin, 'Then say yes.'

'If we're going to a hotel, I didn't bring any decent clothes.'

'And I haven't got any, so we're equal. But damn it, I suppose it means I'll have to shave. Can we pop by the cottage so that I can shower? We need to get our skates on.'

Rory grabbed his mobile and called to confirm the meeting.

They argued about who should do the washing up, and Stephanie won by default as Rory remembered he had to go and tend to his injured bird. As she stood there in the shack with her hands in the bowl, she reflected that it was a very domestic situation, and she felt exceedingly comfortable with it. Surely something that felt so right couldn't be all illusion?

Rory must have felt so, too, for as he strode in, slamming the door behind him, he gave her a quick peck on the cheek in passing, almost without thought.

She put her hand to her cheek where warmth lingered.

'Shall we go in my car?' she asked.

'For my image?'

'No, conversation – or lack of it, in your truck.'

'Maybe that's why I like it.'

'If you're afraid of my driving, I understand.'

'I love your driving. It keeps me interested.'

She smiled.

They made the short drive up to the cottage, and Rory refused to be drawn into what the meeting was about.

'It's business,' he said.

'If I'm standing in as your secretary, it won't be secret for much longer.'

'No, but the suspense will keep you on your toes.'

While Rory was showering, she decided to put a clean t-shirt on, at least, and while she was in the bedroom brushing her wind-knotted hair, there was a knock at the door.

'My shirts are in there, do you mind?'

'Come on in, I'm decent.'

He wasn't.

Still damp from the shower, his face cleanly shaven, and nothing but a small towel wrapped around his middle, he was deliciously un-decent.

Stephanie stared.

Covered in his working clothes she'd

known he was brawny, but without clothes she could see that, unlike her, he didn't carry an inch of extraneous fat. Faintly browned still from the summer, his broad shoulders were ridged with muscle, his robust legs covered in a down of sandy hair.

She flushed faintly at the belt of desire that grabbed her, hoping he couldn't guess the errant wish to see the tiny towel fall. He grabbed a shirt from a drawer, and marched back out, apparently oblivious to her confusion.

Back downstairs, she realised he'd lied about not having decent clothes. Well, not lied exactly, but it was the kind of throwaway remark that didn't tell the whole story. His jeans were clean, and over a fine lawn shirt and traditional tie he pulled a fine wool tweed jacket that was comfortable with use. He had all the panache of a billionaire wearing casuals.

'Will I do?' he asked.

'That depends on who you're trying to impress. But I seriously didn't bring anything other than t-shirts.'

'You'd look lovely in anything.' He stopped short. 'No, not lovely; inexpressibly beautiful.

To Stephanie's consternation crossed the floor between them, leaned over and dropped a butterfly-light kiss on her open lips. It wasn't enough. So much for caveman tactics and brute force, she thought wryly – never there when you most wanted them.

But the look in his eyes was warm with pleasure. 'I just wanted to see if you were real.'

All the way to Plymouth, Rory was silent, obviously mulling something over.

'Sorry,' he said at one stage. 'My mind is kind of busy.'

'Just direct me when we get to the city.'

As they approached the outskirts, Rory came out of his reverie.

'Here we go. Take the outside lane.'

'Are you going to let me in on the big secret before the meeting. If you don't, I might just go shopping instead.'

'Blackmail?'

'Obviously the only way.'

'Take the next slip road.'

'OK.'

'I'm going to turn the boatyard into a small Marina with all the up-market facilities the yachting crowd can't seem to do without.'

'What?' She was surprised. 'That's the big project Jimmy was hinting at? Are you selling out, then, to this Corporation? I thought you didn't want to sell?'

'I'm not selling. They wanted to knock everything down to make way for a holiday complex, which wouldn't have done much for the town, and also would have brought an influx of people who would change the whole ethos of the town. This is a funded project that will bring in sailors and fishermen – not the same as the traditional fishermen, obviously, but a clientele base that won't actually harm the structure of the town.'

'It must be costing thousands.'

'Millions. Ok, take a left here.'

'But where will it all come from?'

'There are agencies that deal in funding this type of development. Pension funds, large corporations. They have money that needs to be invested, and I've persuaded them we'll get a good return on a deep-water mooring.'

'Will you?'

'I hope so. Look, that's the hotel. There's VIP parking by the main entrance.'

'But how on earth can you afford it?'

'The land alone is worth over a million just because of where it's sited. People have been trying to get in there for years, I told you.'

'Oh.'

When he had said he wouldn't be broke if he sold the land she hadn't realised he meant that kind of money.

'The development itself provides security. Should we go bankrupt, it will be sold on to another investor with the experience to make it work, and the investing companies will have a bad investment to their credit.

'What about you?'

'I will lose pretty much everything. But I didn't venture into this lightly. I've spent years doing surveys of yachting trends, seeing how the existing marinas function. In the unlikely event of meltdown, I have retained independent ownership of the boat yard itself. It will have to be rebuilt to fit in with the marina image, of course.'

'And what about deep-water moorings?'

We'll have to dredge a channel through the estuary. I don't own the bay, but I'll have a leasehold to maintain and rent out the moorings generated by the marina; in return, the marina will fund the maintenance of the harbour wall.'

'And the council will go along with it?'

'You bet your life, they will. It will bring a lot of money in, and most of the council are local shop or hotel owners,' he said, adding sarcastically, 'and they look after their own interests first.'

'What about the fishermen?'

She pulled in beside a polished silver Jaguar.

'Ah, James is here already. The fishing fraternity is torn. They've been offered free safe mooring in the winter months, as long as they're genuinely fishing. If they take advantage of the pleasure trade, and start taking out diving groups and pleasure trips, then they'll pay like everyone else. At the moment they don't see that happening, but it will.'

He shrugged. 'The locals have mixed feelings. Excited at the development, sad at the change.'

His face hardened for a moment.

'People get maudlin, but the old days are gone. There's no living for a small fisherman any longer, and in Townsea, without the fishing trade, my trade is dying, too. I'm not a martyr, and I'm not going to go down with the ship. I had two options – sell or to develop. If I sell, outsiders have total control, they'll cream what they can from the development and be damned to the locals. If I develop, at least I can do it with some degree of care. One day the locals might look back just with nostalgia, and not bitterness.'

'As you do.'

'I don't live in cloud cuckoo land. I remember the hard times. Believe it or not, father would say he wasn't hungry so that I could eat a full meal. Things go full circle – these days most kids think they're hard done by because they don't have the latest mobile phone.'

'So, the kids fit into your scheme?'

'I intend to let the town have some benefit from the influx of wealth. Let the yachties pay in the summer, so the local kids have a place to go through the winter. The solicitors didn't like that a bit.'

Stephanie reached for his hand.

'You won, though.'

'We'll find out in a moment,' he said reticently, 'but it seems like it.'

Rory's hand squeezed hers. 'Ready to improve my image?'

'It doesn't need improving,' she said. 'And I'll tell that to anyone so who says different!'

'That's it,' Rory said admiringly. 'We'll go in guns blazing.'

From reception they were shown to the dining suite, where they had a table near a vast picture window.

James turned out to be a dapper, elderly man with fine white hair. The twinkle in his eye suggested a sense of humour. He stood to greet both Rory and Stephanie with real enthusiasm, a hand for each.

'My dears, welcome,' he said, then to Stephanie, 'Rory said you're his secretary?'

'I've been a PA for quite a few years, now. Highly computer literate, good with statistics, and excellent at detecting bullshit. I haven't decided whether to work for Rory, yet. He has some further persuading to do.'

James was amused.

'When Rory said he was bringing a secretary, I assumed he'd acquired some school-girl, but you obviously have a wealth of experience. I didn't think he had that much sense. There's a lot of donkey work that he's been avoiding for the sake of picking up a mouse.'

'Self-confessed dinosaur,' Rory agreed. 'Good with boats and a sander.'

James assessed Stephanie with professional consideration. 'We shouldn't need to hire a model for the advertising. You'll do fine, if you don't mind me saying so. After signing, our next job will be to get some advertising on the go, and you two will look well together. If you can stump up a pair of heels, it will be all the better.'

She caught Rory's glance.

'I can do heels when I have to. Just not all the time.'

'Ok,' James said. 'Let's eat first. We're meeting the solicitors upstairs in an hour or so.'

Stephanie was in a different head space.

Just a few days ago she'd come to Townsea seeking Tass, but she'd met Rory and fallen for him in some indefinable kind of way, and now she was acting as his secretary.

Was this make-believe, or real?

Would she really give up her job to work for Rory? The thought wasn't unattractive. As he said, she'd live by the sea. In the summer she could dive and sail and swim without it being a mammoth effort. But where would she live? And how could it possibly work if she was going to have a relationship with him, and it fell through?

She stopped eating, a fork hanging by her lips.

Had she really just thought that?

Rory stopped eating, too. 'Steph, is anything the matter?'

'No, everything's fine. I just had a strange thought, that's all.'

'Want to share.'

'Not at all.'

He smiled. 'I'll worm it out of you later.'

James glanced from Rory to Stephanie. His jaw visibly dropped. 'Rory, you secretive devil! When's the happy day?'

'A bit previous,' Rory said. 'I haven't asked her, yet.'

'And I haven't answered the question he hasn't asked.'

'Ah, well, congratulations for the future.'

He tipped his glass and took a tiny sip.

During the meeting, Stephanie saw James Mayhew-Jones in his element. Quite what his role was, she wasn't sure, but he had his finger on the pulse. The sharply-suited money men who arrived with the assumption they would take control, didn't.

Stephanie had agreed to come with Rory for a variety of reasons; a sense of repaying a debt, because she wanted to spend the day with him, and not least, rampant curiosity. What she hadn't anticipated, was the pleasure at which she would listen to the conversation.

Her previous experience of secretarial work had been less than glamorous; consisting of writing badly constructed letters dictated by directors with inflated egos.

She'd attended management meetings and financial discussions many times in, but just to take notes and produce action lists. She had never been interested in what was being proposed, and had never been asked for her opinion, as Rory did from time to time, turning to her for approval over things about which she knew nothing. He was animated with enthusiasm and, she realised, wanted to share it with her.

His broad finger traced across the plans as he explained things, leaning over the stark black and white image of the proposed buildings, floating pontoons, and deep-water berths. She felt a dawning wonder that she was involved at the birth of such a scheme.

Listening with objective curiosity, what came over to her more than anything at all was the level of commitment Rory had put into the project over the last few years. It was, as he said, no instant decision. If he had wanted, he could have just sold the land and moved away quite comfortably, but he hadn't taken the easy option.

The project would take him to his limits both financially and mentally, she imagined, before he would reap the benefits – if it worked. She guessed that the indigent population of Townsea would see it as Rory, seeming to suddenly acquire wealth, taking advantage of this to undermine their heritage. He would become an outcast to the community he was trying to help. Her heart reached out to him, to the self-imposed isolation he would achieve in his home town, at least until the prejudice wore off. And people were quite capable of harbouring prejudice for an inordinate length of time.

He didn't just need a secretary. He needed a friend, someone who would stand by him through a traumatic time, trust him, love him, and prove it in little ways to keep him going.

Stephanie didn't know if she was that person.

Rory was on a high, though. He talked all the way back to Townsea, bit his tongue in the supermarket, and got going again on the way back to the cottage, then finally, when he got out, Stephanie reached up and touched his lips softly with her finger. 'Stop,' she said.

Rory burst into the most spontaneous laughter she'd ever heard, and he picked her up under her arms and swung her around exuberantly in a full circle.

'But, I've done it,' he cried exuberantly. 'Do you realise, it's actually going to happen?'

Stephanie felt a buzz of excitement, then as he lowered her, the laughter died. 'Even now, it's not set in stone,' she reminded him.

'I refuse to be deflated. Let tomorrow bring what it will. Today I've won a victory, and –' he paused mid-flow, then added in a more subdued tone, 'I'm so glad you were there to share it with me. It would have been a lonely victory, otherwise.'

He released her, and walked her to the door.

'Let me get some clean clothes for tomorrow, and you can drive me back down into town.'

She started to speak, paused, then spat it

out. 'Would you stay here?'

'Do you want me to stay?'

His hesitancy sat strangely on his big frame.

'It's a sleepover,' she said dryly.

'I didn't think anything else. Well, maybe I thought just a little bit.'

'There are three bedrooms. Besides, I bought something to make a light dinner with, and a bottle of wine, I doubt you noticed. I thought it seemed like a bottle-of-wine sort of occasion.'

'Then I'd love to. It would seem a bit flat, going back to the hut on my own after all this excitement.'

Chapter 7

Later Stephanie couldn't recall in detail how the evening disappeared. After a spurned offer to assist with cooking, Rory sat and mulled over some draft paperwork, lifting his eyes now and then to where she pottered about in the kitchen. She was preparing a salad and baking a piece of smoked salmon in butter, basking in the glow of his euphoria.

She was also used to being on her own, and it was strangely companionable to have him simply *there.* She'd suggested he should go and watch TV, but he said he'd rather watch her.

Now and again she turned and met his smile with a small acknowledgement, enjoying his presence without need to vocalize the fact.

And when the meal was over, they moved into the living room, cuddling tumblers of wine. Rory sat on the settee, and Stephanie curled up in the chair by the window staring out often into the darkness. This time he was there to drive away any night demons who peered in to disturb her.

At what stage she left the chair and ended up curled in the crook of Rory's body, she wasn't sure. She had vague recollections of him walking over and picking her up as she drowsed like a contented cat, then holding her as a mother holds a child; but later, huddled against the cold in the double bed, she found herself intensely alone.

Aware of him in the next room, sleep fled, and with that rude awakening the monsters of the night crept insidiously in. The storm brewed in her mind. The near-tragedy on the cliff became a recurring image, and the suffocating memory of Tass's drowning stilled her breathing with panic on more than one occasion.

Knowing he was so close, she desperately wanted Rory to walk in and hold her, send away the bad dreams with his solid presence, but the consequences of that action would be far reaching.

She couldn't sleep with Rory until such time that she was sure it was right, and if that time didn't arise, then she would never sleep with him. He would not become the fading memory of a few nights' loving, because he wasn't that kind of man, and she didn't want to ruin a possible relationship by a thoughtless act. She realised that for him sex was an extension of loving, a small part of a larger pledge to a whole future, and she wasn't ready to make such commitment.

But she imagined him lying in his bed, his robust body naked between the sheets, wondering if he lay curled in sleep, or was gazing into the darkness in wakefulness, as she was. Tass's death still presented a thorny barrier, and between that and the exquisite pain of Rory's presence, she tossed and turned for what seemed like hours before sinking into a troubled sleep.

When she awoke it was a cold morning with a clear blue sky. The clouds had finally blown over, and the weak warmth of a distant sun brightened her spirits. She stretched luxuriously, realising she must, after all, have slept.

Rory didn't stir as she slipped on some clothes, crept downstairs and stood outside in the early morning dew. She had forgotten how good it was to wake to the smell of wet grass and a salt sea air. In the distance the sea sparkled between the red cliffs that bounded the bay, and to the east the remains of the old look-out station stood out starkly against the blue sky.

The thought of returning to the daily

routine of traffic jams between home and the office, and the continual sound of street noise, thinly filtered during the day by a double-glazed window, seemed unreal and remote.

The cottage had a narrow garden bounded by a small stone wall and was filled with the dying remains of summer flowers. Someone had once loved that small patch of ground, but it was obvious that little real work had been done there for some time. Not having had access to a garden since moving from her parents' home, Stephanie bent and separated the tangled vegetation, removing some of the rotting remains to clear a space for the winter Jasmine she spied by the wall.

'What's that?'

The unexpected sound of his voice made her jump. Rory slouched casually behind her, his shirt-tails hanging out, his hands in his pockets. How long he had been watching, she didn't know.

'What? The Jasmine?'

'No, what you were singing.'

She blushed faintly as his sleepy, sexy eyes indolently perused her from head to toe, and lingered on her muddy hands.

'I didn't realise I was singing.'

'Humming, I should have said. Don't apologise for being happy. Do you like gardening?'

'No. At least, I don't know. I wasn't interested when I lived at home, but I've never had a garden to find out. I just came out to wake up properly and felt sorry for the Jasmine, choked by all that weed.'

Rory put his head to one side.

'I wouldn't know a Jasmine if it leapt out and bit me. Mother would be horrified if she could see the garden like this, you know. She was always pottering about doing something to it. She hasn't come back here since father died, and I spend far too much time at the yard.'

'Because you need to earn the money. That's something that happens to all of us.'

He shook his head. 'Because it's lonely up here. Down at the yard there's usually somebody passing by – even if they're just wandering through to walk the dog.'

'Don't you mind them wandering through?'

'Of course not. I'm retaining the access through to the river bank, though, for dog walkers and twitchers. I don't see why those who like nature should be denied the pleasure just because a few rich people want privacy on their yachts.'

She glanced around at the silent, rolling landscape. 'It must have been lonely for your mother up here, too.'

'The other two cottages were lived in when I was young, there were other mothers and children around. It wasn't lonely then. Total solitude is something else, though – solitary confinement. You'd kill for a kind word, or any word, for that matter. I'm hoping I can buy the whole row eventually, knock this cottage into the next one, it's hardly big enough for a family these days, and as for the end one, we could keep it as guest accommodation.'

'You'd like a family then,' Stephanie asked, shyly.

He bent and kissed her fleetingly on the cheek. 'Don't you? It's what makes the world go around. Do you want some coffee?'

When he said *we,* perhaps it hadn't been a slip of the tongue, after all.

It was during the slim breakfast of coffee and toast that Stephanie realised Rory was working up to something.

He fiddled thoughtfully with the cutlery on the table before finally broaching it. 'I suppose you still want to see Thomas Purdie?'

She gave him a level gaze. 'Yes.'

'You won't reconsider?'

'If you tell me the truth I won't need to.'

He sighed fractionally. 'I thought you'd say

163

that. I didn't go and ask him – forewarned is forearmed. He won't even open the door if he knows we're coming.'

Stephanie felt slightly guilty for insisting in going there, no longer sure of her own motives. Two days ago, it would have been to offer unwanted condolences, now it was a quest for the truth.

'I'm sorry,' she said in a low voice. 'I've got to know, because otherwise...'

'Otherwise?' he prompted gently.

'Otherwise Tass will forever stand between us.'

He gave a regretful sigh and stood up.

'I'd hoped we were strong enough to get past that.'

Stephanie carried the plates to the sink.

'We can't start a relationship with a secret. It would be an open wound. It would fester and destroy us. I won't take that chance.'

'You could try trusting me.'

'It's not that simple. If you trusted me, you'd tell me what really happened.'

'I wasn't there, I don't know.'

'You're prepared to let me go that easily?'

'I'm not prepared to let you go at all, but if I told you anything, it would just be gossip or supposition, and my conscience won't allow me to do that. You can assess the facts and make your own conclusions, as we all did who knew the people involved, and when you've done that, you'll have to tell me if there is still a secret mouldering between us, because I won't know.'

'You're exasperating.'

'I know.' Rory smiled, and she could see the love in his eyes. 'And you have to do what you have to do. So, the best way is just to go and knock on Thomas's door. You'd better be prepared for a rebuff, though.'

'And if he won't talk to me?'

'Then I'll have to stop you leaving me some other way. I don't intend to let Tass keep me from the woman I want to marry.'

She was startled. 'And you decided that, when?'

'Oh, months ago. Now I'm sure.'

Her heart somersaulted as his words sent a flutter of yearning through her body, but she made her voice acerbic to cover her consternation.

'I don't see how you can be, when you hardly know me.'

'I know enough to be sure.'

'Well I don't know you.'

'I think you do. You have to believe what you already know.'

'Do you always have an answer for everything?'

'Pretty much.'

Contrary to expectations, Thomas was not at his house, he was finally located at the harbour-side, where he sat mending some nets in the chill breeze. So much for Jimmy's assertation that he would never go back to sea, Stephanie thought. His cruel mistress was still the sea, though she'd taken his child from him.

Thomas looked older than his fifty-eight years; his small wiry frame bent by excesses of wind and weather, his fingers gnarled, and his face wizened beneath the blue drill cap. It was only when he looked up and saw them standing there, that she saw a resemblance to Tass in his moss-green eyes.

It ran in the family.

She saw his relaxed face stiffen as he realised there was to be yet another intruder into his life, another reporter, maybe, to rake up the muck which was best left undisturbed.

He scowled and bent furiously over his nets, trying to ignore them, determined not to be routed from his position by their intrusion.

Rory made to speak, but Stephanie waved her hand to silence him. She walked forward and crouched down beside where the old man sat on an upturned crate. He didn't acknowledge her presence.

'I was Tass's girlfriend,' she said finally.

'You and a hundred others,' he replied callously, his fingers moving quickly and precisely over the torn loops.

'I know; but I hoped I'd be his last.'

'You were a fool.'

'You don't choose who you love. At the time I had no choice, and I waited for him to call me. When he didn't, I came back, and found out that he was dead. I want you to know I'm sorry, that's all.'

'Sorry.' He gave a bitter laugh. 'You shouldn't have wasted your time.'

'I know it doesn't make anything any easier, but I *am* sorry. Tass was a wonderful person to be with. Wayward and foolish, maybe, but he was young. He would have grown up eventually.'

'Wayward and foolish.' He seemed to muse over her choice of words. Then his eyes slashed to Rory who stood some distance back, staring out to sea. There was a querulous note barely discernible in the anger. 'Why did you bring her here?'

Rory acknowledged his question with a shrug, followed by, 'I tried to tell her not to interfere, but she has a mind of her own.'

'I just wanted to know what happened, that's all.'

'If you want to know, go and read the

papers. There's enough gossip there to keep you amused for a month.' Thomas's hostility burst like a bubble. Suddenly, he was just a sad, old man, trying to stop the tears which moistened his eyes. 'Go away,' he said. 'Just go away and leave me alone. Tass is dead, may God forgive him, and that's the end on it.'

He turned his back purposefully, and continued to work, but Stephanie saw the gnarled hands falter and begin to shake.

She rose silently and backed off.

Rory straightened and walked silently alongside. When they were out of earshot, he said, 'That went well.'

'Sarcasm isn't helpful.'

'So, what now?'

'I want to see the papers.'

It was Rory's turn to be exasperated. 'Don't you ever let up?'

Upset by her experience with Thomas, Stephanie gave vent to her spleen. 'I didn't ask you to go with me! Go and play with your boats or something. I'll do it on my own.'

'The newspaper office is in Breminster.'

'All I need is an internet café.'

'That'll be in Breminster, too. The one in Townsea is closed for the winter.'

Rory thrust his hands in his pockets and scowled, then gave her directions. 'In

Breminster, go down the main street, where we walked. Turn right just past the church, and you'll find a big car park.'

'Thank you.' Her tone was grudging. 'What are you going to do?'

'Go and play with my boats.'

Stephanie almost giggled at the sullen tone. His eyes slid sideways, his mouth twitching in response.

'If you're going to Breminster, will you do something for me?'

'What?'

'Buy me a computer.'

'What for?'

'Secretarial work. Accounts. Everything.'

She frowned. 'I don't know if I want to work for you, Rory. In fact, I'm almost sure I don't.'

'But I'll still need a computer,' he said, 'Even if I have to do the letters myself, and I wouldn't have the faintest idea what to buy.'

'You'll need a printer too. One with a scanner.'

'Goddamn! I knew that was the thin end of the wedge.'

'And you'll have to get broadband.'

He glared. 'You're enjoying this, aren't you?'

'No. How much do you want to spend, and how shall I pay for it?'

He shrugged. 'Get what's best for the job. Something that will last a few years. I'll phone them up and give my credit card details.'

'Where should I go?'

'There's only one office suppliers. On the main street, you can't miss it. Get something that I can understand.'

'They don't make steam computers.'

'Vixen.'

But there was warmth in his voice and his arm snaked around her shoulders and stayed there.

They were wandering back up the lane towards the boatyard when a car beeped its horn behind them. They flattened themselves back against the wall to let it squeeze past. Rory raised his free hand in greeting to the driver. 'This will be all over town tonight,' he said, giving her a slight hug.

'Do you mind?'

'Hell, it will give people something to gossip about. I don't think I've been seen with a woman in the last few years. Rumour has it that I've got a boyfriend in Breminster.'

'Have you?'

He gave a shout of laughter. 'No, I haven't. Are you going to make us a meal tonight, too?'

'Do you want me to?'

'If you're going to run off at any moment, I have to make the most of your talents now. After the stew the other day I thought, girl's got talent. She can cook like my mother.' Stephanie thumped him. 'Ow. Then after the Salmon, I thought, I'd better see if I can keep her.'

'So, you need a cook.'

'And a housekeeper.'

'And a maid?'

'Only if she does night duty. I was freezing last night, thinking about you lying in my nice warm bed.'

'I'd have been quite happy in one of the other rooms. It was you who decided.'

'More fool me. But maybe not. It would be much warmer with two.'

She stopped short and faced him. 'OK. What if I said yes? You can sleep in your bed with me, tonight?' He looked gobsmacked, at a loss for words. 'See, it's nothing to joke about. I've never, ever done one-night stands.'

'Nor have I,' he said.

'I'm not joking.'

'Nor was I.'

She glared. 'And before you hit me with it, that time with Tass was – different. I'd never done anything like that before. And I enjoyed it.'

'That's a smack in the teeth.'

'It's the truth. Now, go and play boats. I'm going to buy a computer and do some research. I'll see you back at the cottage, around six?'

He stopped, slammed his heels together, presented an immaculate salute, then ambled into the yard without looking back.

Stephanie found the computer shop first, and in the window was a sign that there was internet surfing available, which made life easy. The shop could have been anywhere in the world, wallpapered with screens that flickered the same images. She winced at the sensory overload. But at least there was no piped music.

'Hi. What can I do for you?'

'Hi. The sign says you have internet?"

The young man behind the counter was having difficulty tearing his eyes from the screen he'd been working on. She caught a glimpse before he killed the screen. He'd obviously been blasting aliens out of the sky.

'Follow me,' he said.

'But first I need buy a computer,' she added.

His attitude switched from distant to overtly friendly in a second. He walked to a wall of computers and began a sales patter designed to impress and probably confuse.

She held her hand up. 'Stop.'

He stopped, mid-word.

'I don't know what gave you the impression that I'm a gullible idiot. I need a computer for work, not gaming, it doesn't need to look like the control panel for the Enterprise. It needs the standard keyboard and mouse. I don't want an enormous monitor, but I do need it to be large enough to see AutoCAD plans in detail. I don't need high def speakers, or any speakers come to that; headphones with a mic will be fine. I want a desktop package with writing and spreadsheet capabilities, and I'd like to you load it while I'm on the internet. And if you'd be so good as to find some freeware that will read AutoCAD drawings, that would be most helpful.'

She pointed to a mid-priced grey box. 'I guess that one will do the trick?'

He grinned. 'I guess it will.'

Stephanie followed him to the internet computer and spent the next hour trawling. She didn't find much more than she had been told already.

Tass's death had made front page headlines in the local papers, *Local Lad in Scuba Drowning Disaster*, and there were a few knock-on articles in national papers, which she hadn't noticed at the time. But as they'd used Tass's real name, William Purdie, she wouldn't have made the connection, anyway, except for a photo that must have been taken a few years back, when he was a skinny teenager. His character and charisma weren't obvious from the image, and she barely recognised him.

The coverage was at the same time both banal and critical. On one hand they praised the virtues of those who had gone to make the wreck safe, and on the other slated those who indulged in such dangerous pastimes: deep sea diving was apparently costing the tax-payers thousands of pounds. The woman who had reported it, Stephanie realised, knew absolutely nothing, and had just latched onto all the sentimental or contentious angles possible.

It annoyed her.

Rescues within the world of dangerous sports could only be carried out by those experienced in that sport, and who largely volunteered. Even the lifeboats were self-funded, manned by volunteers, and they rescued tax-paying idiots on plastic blow-up toys by the thousands every year.

She found a small article covering the inquest, which had passed a verdict of misadventure and accidental death.

The most disturbing thing she found was a blog discussing Jimmy's inheritance, and the possibility of his having murdered Tass. It had been argued to death, with varying degrees of intelligence and accuracy. The international blog, on a diving website, pretty much suggested Jimmy had literally got away with murder.

Everyone had loved Tass. No-one knew Jimmy.

Compassion for Jimmy welled up inside her.

You never really did live past people's beliefs, even if they were wrong. She felt sure Tass's cousin had been honest with her, and she didn't have the slightest doubt that he was innocent of the charge, despite his possible windfall inheritance.

And that was all.

The elusive truth was not going to be discovered online, she realised. It was only going to be discovered through chatting to the people involved. And it seemed they had clammed up together, in true community solidarity.

Even Rory.

At the till, her reddened eyes must have told their own story, for the youth who had been serving her with the computer asked if she was OK. She'd seen him surreptitiously glancing at the screen.

'Oh, I'm fine. I was just checking up about a friend who died.'

'You knew Tass?

She nodded. 'I only found out by accident, a couple of days ago. It shocked me, to be honest.'

'It shocked all of us at the time. He was the life and soul of Townsea. His family seems bugged by bad luck.'

Stephanie stopped short. 'What do you mean?'

'Oh, just that both boys lost their mothers early, then Tass's father fucked off and was never seen again, and after all that, Tass dying in that crazy way. It just about sent Thomas over the edge. When Martin Purdie dies, that's Jimmy's father, out of three whole families there's only going to be the two of them left – Jimmy and his uncle Thomas.'

He sounded genuinely saddened, as if he knew them well. But then, that's the way these small towns worked. Everyone knew everyone else's business.

'You said *when* Martin dies?

'He's ill, didn't you know? Not expected to live out the year. Thomas will be the last of the three brothers. He never married, but there was some talk of a broken engagement many years ago, and he never looked at another woman, and then to take in his brother's son, only to see him drown.'

He shook his head.

'Shouldn't happen to one family, should it?'

He was right, Stephanie thought. So much pain, so much sadness. No wonder Thomas had resented her interference. And no wonder Janet, Jimmy's girlfriend had been so antagonistic.

The young man was dismantling the computer. He put all the leads in a bag.

'So, how would you like to pay?'

'It's for Rory Banner. He said he'd phone ahead?'

The sales assistant's eyes lit up, probably with the anticipation of more gossip.

'He sure did. Rory coming into the twenty-first century, though! That'll be a first!'

She raised her brows. He must know Rory well. 'I also want a pile of cardboard wallets, a stapler, a hole punch, some ring binders and some sticky labels.'

His expression was urging her to say more, but she merely added, 'So, if you're happy about the finance, I'll go and get my car.'

'Great, great. It'll take a couple of minutes. I'll give you the credit card receipt to take back.'

'Thank you.'

As she went to collect her car, she was beset by a kind of guilt for even reading all that raked-over dirt on the internet. She had no business interfering. Rory was right, after all. She'd achieved nothing but harm with her stupid questions – all of which Rory had already answered; and yet, there was still a niggle at the back of her mind.

He'd almost admitted that something else had happened, something other than what had been reported. He'd known she would find nothing when he'd directed her to the internet café.

Back at the cottage she threw a casserole in the oven and let it get on with itself while she emptied Rory's overflowing box full of papers, and the contents of his brief-case, onto the carpet. The least she could do for him before she left was to put it all into some semblance of order.

She thought about his request that she do his secretarial work, but it seemed unworkable. How on earth could she be a secretary to someone who wanted her to be more than that?

Everyone had been telling her to leave them alone to mourn Tass, and at this moment it seemed they were right. She'd come to find him. He was gone, and she'd been released from the desperate attraction she'd been harbouring for him. She should leave, distance herself from both Tass and Rory before making her next move.

The light gradually faded, and it seemed like only moments before she heard Rory's pick-up growling up the hill. She glanced up. It was nearly seven.

He knocked and came in without waiting for her to answer.

'It's only me. Blimey,' he said, mildly. 'I hope you know what you're doing. I knew where everything was, before.'

'It's sorted,' she explained, 'I just need to put it into the separate folders, then there's just a small pile of things that need your attention. I'll put notes on them all. But I think you'll need to set up one of the bedrooms as an office and get a telephone extension for the internet connection.'

He went over and stared at the computer.

'Looks like a computer,' he said.

She grinned. 'I'll give you a crash course. Show you the on-button. Oh, and you need a filing cabinet for this lot really. It's not going to get any easier once things get moving.'

'Why didn't you order one?'

'I thought I'd spent enough of your money

already.'

'Woman in a million,' he said, bending to give her a kiss. 'I'll phone for one tomorrow. It looks as though you've been at this for hours. Can I smell something very interesting cooking?'

His stomach gave an audible growl.

'There's a beef casserole in the oven. I hope you like it. It was the easiest thing to cook, and left me free to get on with this.'

He pulled a bottle of wine from the pocket of his storm-jacket.

'The mess can take care of itself. Come and have a drink with me.'

'I'm going to put it away first while I still know what I've put where.'

'Dare I ask how you got on today, apart from sorting out my paperwork?' he asked blandly.

She sat back on her heels. 'You know damn well I wouldn't find anything that matters, and a lot which should never have been printed.'

'Of course. But you had to find out for yourself. I expect it helped in some way.'

Stephanie slumped. 'Maybe.'

'But it didn't answer your questions?' She grimaced. 'I'll take that as a no, then.'

He walked away. She heard the cork pop, and the chink of glasses. She slammed the next lot of papers into a labelled cardboard wallet venomously, adding it to the growing pile.

He sighed. 'I think you need that glass of wine.'

'I'm fine.'

'Yes, it sounds like it,' he said, seating himself on the sofa. She gasped as he bent and heaved her up onto his lap.

'You can't do that,' she said tightly, freezing.

'What can't I do?' he asked reasonably. 'Now just try relaxing. This is like cuddling a plastic doll. Not that I've had any experience.'

She almost giggled, but annoyance still warred against the natural inclination to slump into his shoulder. 'People can be really vicious.'

'They can.'

'Jimmy was exonerated, but everyone thinks he did it.'

'They do. Doesn't mean he did.'

'Poor Jimmy.'

She found herself crying into his shoulder. He just held her, his arms tightening, comforting her wordlessly, as one would a child.

'I'm sorry,' Stephanie finally hiccupped.

'You'll ruin my best jacket if it carries on much longer.'

'It's waterproof.'

'So it is. Well, it was once.'

'Are you going to put me down, now?'

'Nope.'

Stephanie frowned. 'I'm O.K. now. Really.'

'You may be, but I'm quite comfortable.'

'The dinner will be ruined.'

He stood and dumped her on her feet. 'Now that would break my heart. I'll just go and get cleaned up.'

He paused at the door and looked back. 'I love you too much to let you be unhappy.'

She was shocked. 'You don't know what you're saying. You've only known me a few days.'

'I've known you forever. You just didn't find your way home before now.'

He left a vast warm space in the lounge, and Stephanie wondered how he could have filled her mind so completely, so surely in such a short time. His presence remained with her, even when he wasn't there; and when he was there, it was just comfortable, as if he'd been in her life forever.

That was scarier than her infatuation with Tass.

But in spite of the underlying uncertainty, she hummed to herself as she removed the casserole from the oven and set it on the table.

If this was truly love, then it was up to her to remove Tass from between them. What was past and gone shouldn't be allowed to stop her from walking forward into a new life, a new beginning.

When Rory descended down the small stairs, in three bounds, freshly washed and brushed, she couldn't help her small smile of pride at the sight. Somewhere in the back of her mind she quite liked the idea that this was her man and she was his.

He looked so wholesome, so perfect, she was continually amazed at the way he seemed engrossed in her, despite her present tendency to drip like a tap all over him, at the least opportunity, about another bloke.

'Let me at it,' he said, sniffing the air, then frowned, staring. 'What on earth is that?'

'Casserole. With a suet pastry topping, sort of like dumplings that have gone browned.'

She cut into it, and the juices burst through the crust with a tantalising scent of herbs.

'My mother used to make this when I was little.'

'I can see you having to make it a lot in the future,' he said, eyes gleaming. 'Our kids are going to love it.'

He poured out more wine as she served.

'When are you going to phone your boss?'

She paused. 'What?'

'To tell him you've found another job.'

'I'm not. I haven't. I'm just helping to sort you out a bit, to use your own words. Tomorrow morning I'll put the computer together and do those few letters for you from the meeting. Then I'm going to go back home and assimilate what has happened before I make any stupid decisions that I'll regret later.'

'No, you're not,' he said. 'All my life I've been looking for a woman who can cook, and now I've found her, I'm not about to let her out of my sight. The fact that you can type, too, is just a bonus.'

'Don't pressure me, Rory. Just eat.'

'I'm not pressurising.'

'Well what would you call it, then,' she said, half smiling, half exasperated.

'Coercion.' He began to tuck in. 'My God, this is good. Ball and chain, if necessary.'

'I'm going back.'

'I'll let your tyres down if you try.'

'Will you be serious?'

'I am.'

'You're worrying me.'

He reached across the table and held her hand for a moment.

'Sorry. I wouldn't hurt you for the world; but I promise if you leave, I'll follow, unless you tell me now, categorically, that there's something about me that repulses you.'

Stephanie like the feel of his broad hand wrapped around her own, but he released her all too soon and sat back with a satisfied, smug look.

'There. You can't.'

He lifted his glass. 'To our future?'

She lifted her glass to touch it gently to his.

'To the future, whatever that might be.'

'And happiness,' Rory said, a soft light in his eye. 'Being content with what life gives you even if it wasn't what you planned.'

Stephanie was slightly scathing. 'What, when you're planning so much! What's it all for, then, the hassle, the trauma of all this development? Wouldn't you be better off leaving well alone?'

'What, everything comes to those who wait? I don't know what idiot coined that phrase. Contentment is not complacency. You can't sit back on your laurels and wait for happiness, you have to go out and find it. What I meant was, the philosophy of learning not to be bitter about the things that happen unplanned – which they often do.'

'Whose philosophy is that?'

'Mine.'

'You're making me feel very naive and stupid.'

'Don't be daft. You're a wonderful, kind and caring human being. That's why I love you. That's why I am going to fight for you.'

'Besides which, I can cook and type.'

'Well, I don't want any hangers-on in my empire. Multi-tasking is the key.'

'It's going to be an empire, now, is it?'

'My Dad always said, think big.'

Stephanie's brow rose.

Rory's grin broke free. 'You'd better eat your dinner before I lose my self-control.'

She flushed over the wine-glass, the faint glow of desire building up into a flame that curled around her insides. Without the hint of nostalgia, she thought on the crazy nights with Tass, and knew that loving Rory would be a less frenzied experience. How had she come to this in such a short time?

'I jumped into bed with Tass the first day I met him. How can you not *mind* that?'

'You're prevaricating.'

'I know, but I'm also curious.'

'I do mind, but one has to be realistic. The old chestnut *I'd rather be the last than the first* comes to mind.' He gave a grimace. 'Don't forget, I knew Tass since he was a child. Even back then he attracted people like flies. Not just girls, but the boys, too. He had a kind of, I don't know, je ne sais quoi, that made people want to be with him, be his friend, his lover, his satellite. I don't think I ever understood quite what that was.'

She reflected, 'I've been trying to work that out, too. But you weren't affected by it.'

'Wasn't I?'

'But you –'

'Just because I wasn't blind to his faults doesn't mean I didn't enjoy his company.' He paused. 'It was only when you came on the scene that it became personal. Up to that point I hadn't realised how utterly ruthless he was. And heartless.'

'I'm glad I didn't know that.'

'Yes, well.' He sighed. 'Here he is, still between us, eh?'

But he wasn't really, Stephanie thought. The image of Tass-the-unscrupulous had imposed itself over Tass-the-sultry-lover, and it fitted too well. How could she have been so taken in?

Had Rory uttered the smallest persuasion, she would have gone to him that night, but he didn't. They sat and watched a film together curled up on the sofa, Rory leaning into the corner, herself leaning into his shoulder.

He gave her a lingering kiss at the bedroom door, leaving her in doubt as to the depth of his desire, yet he went into the spare toom, closing the door firmly behind him.

Chapter 8

It was only as Stephanie rose out of a deep and contented sleep the next morning, that she realised Rory had given her something no man had ever given her before: uncomplicated companionship.

But still, she knew this time had been too short for the huge decision and commitment he was angling for.

But she had kept her promise.

It wasn't that she no longer mourned Tass. More than that, she couldn't fathom why she'd been with him at all, acting like a randy teenager. The Tass she'd been yearning for had been a figment of her imagination, and how can you mourn someone who had never existed? The real Tass held all the attraction of a mafia boss, glossy on the outside, festering inside, and she guessed that was what he'd been, in his own small-town way. The Townsea mafia thug.

Rory was worth a hundred of him.

And so was Jimmy.

She came downstairs to find a note from Rory. *Sorry, I had to shoot out, hope you had a good sleep, see you for lunch? Here or in town? Let me know.*

She must have slept deeply in the end, she thought. She hadn't heard him creep downstairs, nor heard the pick-up grind into life.

After mooching with a cup of coffee and a piece of toast, she gathered her energy, and finished the sorting and filing that had been interrupted the previous evening.

When her mobile rang, she assumed it was Rory, but it was an unknown number.

'Is that Stephanie Harding?' an unknown female voice asked.

'Yes?'

'Oh, good. The thing is, I'm your mother's next-door-neighbour. She asked me to call. She broke her arm yesterday and is in the General. She's been trying to call you and got worried when she didn't get an answer.'

'I put my phone on silent for the meeting yesterday and forgot to turn it back on. Darn.'

'I've done that so many times! Anyway, I think they're doing an operation today, putting a pin in, or something. I said I'd carry on trying, see if I could get hold of you.'

'Will you be seeing her? It's just that I'm

not in the city and it's going to take a few hours to get back.'

'Not today, love. Send her a text, let her know you're on your way.'

'OK, and thanks.'

She put the phone down, swore, then went up to throw her things hastily into her case. She sent a text to her mother's phone saying she'd be there after lunch. She tried Rory's mobile several times, but there was no answer, and he didn't seem to have an option to leave a message. James had said he wasn't very good with mobiles, and she'd seen the way he threw it down in the hut and left it there when he went out to work.

Why did he think it was called a mobile?

She set a text, telling him she had to go home for family matters, but she'd call. Then she wondered if he'd even work out how to access the message, or even know it was there. Exasperated, she scribbled a note, too, and left it on the pile of filing. If he didn't get the modern version, he'd certainly get the message the old-fashioned way, later.

She took one final look around the place before driving off, wondering if she'd ever see it again.

It was strange how fate had taken a hand.

She'd told Rory she would be leaving, and somehow hadn't known quite how to do it, but it was easy in the end: she threw her bags in the car, climbed in, and drove off.

She had to drive through Townsea to get back onto the main road, and was tempted to stop at the boatyard, but it was a bad idea. Rory would certainly use delaying tactics, and probably even try to persuade her not to go, and she wasn't sure she would resist the lure. But her mother needed her, and that was that.

In a way, this provided the opportunity for her to extricate herself from a situation that had somehow got out of control. It gave her the excuse she needed, to break whatever hold it was that Rory had over her. Truly, she didn't know what that was, and didn't want to leave, but giving herself time to think it all through wasn't a bad thing.

It was a long drive, her divided mind arguing all the way. Was this necessity, in fact, a godsend? Was the interest she felt for Rory real, or had it been simply circumstance? He'd saved her life, so maybe her interest was gratitude? But he was still one of *them*, while she was an outsider. He was throwing lures of a future while holding back some piece of information vital to her understanding of how Tass died. How could there be a future if it was built on a rocky platform?

Was he so keen on her because he was lonely, or, God forbid, she could cook like his mother? Did he want a family and kids just so that his lonely cottage would become warm and welcoming? Or had he truly fallen for her in a big way back in the summer? And had Tass chased her so avidly, so overtly simply because he enjoyed hurting another man, simply because he could?

Was that what Tass had really been like?

And so the argument went, round and round.

After a couple of hours her phone rang, several times in a row. Glancing at the screen, she saw Rory's home number, and events wrote themselves in her mind.

He'd picked up his phone, got her missed calls, maybe her message. He'd shot up to the cottage and discovered it empty, his filing in a neat pile by the new computer, with her note on top. He'd rushed up to the bedroom to see if she'd left anything – proof that she'd be back; and found nothing

Then he'd started to phone.

When the phone went silent, her eyes prickled with tears. The further she drove away from Townsea, the more ephemeral their apparent attraction seemed. She didn't want to hurt him, but he'd be feeling hurt all the same. He must be sitting there, pushing his tousled hair back, wondering whether she would return.

Her note had left room for the possibility.

Space was all she'd asked for. No pressure, just the chance to assess, regroup her feelings, and make her own mind up.

When Stephanie got to the hospital, her mother's eyes lit up. Her arm was encased in bandages from elbow to wrist, strapped to her chest.

'I'm sorry to drag you away from work, darling,' she said, as Stephanie leaned over and dropped a kiss on her cheek. 'Is that why you didn't answer your phone? I was a bit worried; it's not like you.'

'I'd switched it off for a meeting and forgot to turn it on again.'

She sat down on the upright chair beside the bed. Her mother was in a small ward with four other women; one elderly, two of her mother's era, and one teenager. All looked totally bored.

She recalled her one and only stay in hospital with the same degree of frustration. She had wanted to read, but couldn't focus; she had things she wanted to do, but knew even if she had insisted on leaving, she would be too weak to even consider them. Enforced rest, they'd called it, but she didn't recall it being very restful.

'How long have you got to be here?'

'Another day. They did the operation this morning, but they want to put plaster on when the swelling has gone down.'

'So, what happened?'

'Stupid, really. I slipped over in the kitchen. One minute I was standing, the next I was on the floor. I've been considering putting that washable non-slip carpeting in the kitchen, and now I'm going to do it.'

Stephanie grinned. 'That's what's known as shutting the stable door after the horse has bolted.'

'Well, it could easily bolt again. And next time it might not just be my arm. This getting old lark isn't fun.'

When she left the hospital, Stephanie went to the flat, gathered some clean clothes, and made her way to her mother's bungalow, on the other side of the city. She'd bring her Mum home to a clean warm house the next day, have a dinner waiting, and provide moral support for a few days while they worked out how to manage the situation. She wasn't sure, on reflection, whether the moral support was for herself or her Mum.

Whatever, she'd have to stay for a few days,

probably, before going back to work.

She phoned Rory's home number, but there was no answer. He was probably back down at the boatyard by now, probably without his mobile, damn the man, he could at least have an answer facility on his landline.

She phoned her boss's direct line.

'Where the fuck are you?' he asked.

She was taken aback. 'A friend died. It was a bit of a shock. I gave my flat-mate a letter to give to you, and asked her to call to say I wouldn't be in for a bit.'

'I didn't get any message. I've been expecting you in every day this week. Are you on your way?'

Thanks for your understanding, Stephanie thought. But surely Rachel sent the letter in?

'I'm calling to let you know I need a couple more days. My Mum has just broken her arm and I have to –'

He interrupted.

'If you don't get your arse in here today, don't bother. I've got a temp in, and she's a damned sight less argumentative than you.'

The phone went dead. Stephanie gave a stunned laugh. She'd just been sacked? For a woman who was less argumentative? That would stand up well in Court. Or did he mean more accommodating? Her boss had old fashioned notions about a woman's role in the grand scheme of things, and she had challenged that role by not simpering and wearing clothes that exposed a deep cleavage.

Well, it was a problem all right, but she hadn't liked him anyway, so maybe it wasn't such a bad thing.

She went and did some shopping for her Mum, and once she guessed Rachel was home from work, she called her and asked if she'd passed the message on.

'What message?' Rachel said.

Stephanie began to feel disorientated by the coincidences. She didn't believe in fate, but it seemed as if some malicious god had it in for her.

The next day her Mum phoned to say she was plastered and would be allowed out once the surgeon had done his afternoon rounds, after three, so Stephanie decided to go around and talk to her boss first, put things straight.

He couldn't sack her for missing a few days when she'd obviously been grief-stricken, even if he thought he could. But what had passed between them wasn't conducive to a good working relationship, so she would offer to work out her notice, giving him a chance to replace her, and for her to apply for something else, even if it meant going back to temping for a bit.

She was strangely relieved.

She pulled into the car park and made her way up to the sales office. She was about to walk in, when she saw the temp taking notes, leaning forward provocatively, laughing. Despite the distance, the features obscured by two glass doors, she recognised Rachel. Dropping her hand from the handle, she turned and walked away.

It took three trips in her car to collect her stuff from the flat. Once she was finished, with a careful scour of kitchen, bathroom and the shared living room, she phoned her old work number.

'Good morning, Mr Nyam's office,' Rachel said.

'I've vacated the flat,' Stephanie stated. 'I've left the key in the kitchen.'

It took Rachel a long moment to compute that information. 'Steph?' Then her voice rose. 'You can't do that, you've got to give me three months' notice!'

'You've got a month's rent up front. Get the rest from you new boss. Goodbye.'

Slamming the phone down gave her a little satisfaction. The bitch! She and Rachel hadn't exactly become bosom buddies over the couple of years they'd been flatmates, but she hadn't expected that kind of back-handed betrayal. She mentally wished her the best of luck coping with a chauvinistic boss. He'd been nice enough to Stephanie to start with, but it hadn't lasted. What was it with these Directors, with their inflated income and egos? What happened to basic humanity?

Perhaps he and Rachel deserved each other.

In the car, she explained to her Mum some of what had happened, and asked if she minded her moving back in until she could find another job.

'Sweetie, you can stay with me for as long as you like. You don't have to find a flat at all, you know that.'

'I'm going to be a burden if I can't find work.'

'Well, this time, check out the boss carefully. Work for a big firm, darling, they're less likely to employ small minded gits.'

'Mum!'

'Well, I've been thinking that for a while. Perhaps you should find a woman boss.'

'They can be even more horrible,' she said glumly. 'I've meet a few.'

'So, tell me again about this Tass of yours.'

'He wasn't mine, as it turned out. And don't say I told you so, or I'll get a sleeping bag and go to the nearest homeless shelter.'

'I wouldn't dream of it.'

They shared a smile. Then she told her mother of discovering that Tass had died, and how. She left out the bit about nearly going over the cliff, and said nothing about Rory. If she had, her mother would pick relentlessly in the cracks in her story. She could be persistent.

While she was talking her eyes teared-up, and her mother patted her knee with her good hand.

'Oh, love,' she said. 'It's never easy. But that must have been bad, on all counts. Go and get a bottle of wine and we'll get maudlin together, shall we?'

'Mum, you're a brick,' she said, turning into the supermarket car park.

Chapter 9

Stephanie tried to call Rory several times in the weeks following her mother's accident, but he never answered, and didn't return her calls. It was hard to believe that Rory hadn't meant what he said, but time went by and her heart hardened. Eventually, she parked the last vestiges of her dreams, and got on with her life. She decided she'd become an old maid and live on her own with some cats rather than trust anything a bloke said, ever again.

She began the long haul of applying for jobs, wondering whether her last boss, or Rachel, would actively hinder her chances with a bad reference, but her fears proved groundless.

After a few weeks of interviews with people she decided not to work for, she was interviewed at a small factory that specialised in exclusive lingerie. Marie, the owner, had a ready smile, and Stephanie liked her immediately. The feeling must have been mutual as she was offered the job on the spot; and accepted it gratefully.

The work was the same as always: answering phones, typing, filing, arranging meetings, and sorting out venues, shows, and lunches with buyers, but the burden was lessened by Marie's attitude; there was always a please or a thank you at the end of each request.

She attained a level of contentment that was not quite happiness, but within a few of weeks of being there, Marie asked her out of the blue one day, 'Steph, do you enjoy your work?'

She was taken aback. 'Have I done something wrong?'

'It's a simple question.'

The slight smile on Marie's face gave her the courage to be honest. 'Well, ah, secretarial work can be a bit tedious at times, but it's what I expected.'

'A lot tedious for someone with your quick brain, I suspect. Let me show you around the factory floor, meet some of the girls.'

Stephanie wasn't sure where this was leading, and followed nervously down the stairs into a large, light space. Rows of women of all ages were chatting to each other, their hands busily feeding fabrics, with a precision she found fascinating, into machines that hummed and frilled and tucked and stitched.

'Goodness, do they do that all day?'

'All day; but our girls become experts in several processes, and we move them around every few hours to avoid repetitive strain and boredom. The girls call it musical chairs. When the bell goes they all leap up, have a break, and go to their new positions. Some people would call this a sweat shop, but our girls don't usually leave because they're unhappy.'

As they ambled between the rows, Marie spoke to several girls by name, discussing small personal details. They all called her Marie, not Mrs Wickam.

She asked Stephanie, 'Did you never think of going to university?'

'Not really. I'd had enough of education. Mum and Dad tried to persuade me, but I thought I knew best.'

'And without a degree you found there was no room for advancement?'

'That's about right. I never wanted to be a career woman, but being a secretary is, ah, disconcertingly detached from everything. You get to work with the gods, but you know the other gods are only being nice to get through you to the person who employs you.'

Marie laughed out loud. 'I've never heard it put better. How would you like to be a manager?'

'But – I wouldn't know how!'

'Come and meet Mark. He's our self-styled expert in ladies' underwear. Have an informal chat with him, then come back upstairs when you're done.'

When Stephanie finally accepted the post of Under-Manager, Marie called her into the office and handed her a pile of applications for the secretarial post she would be vacating.

'Would you be kind enough to read these and sort out three for interview? I'm more interested in finding someone who fits in, than the one with the fastest typing speed.'

On the top was an application from Rachel.

'Not this one,' she said, and Marie made no objection as she slipped it into the bin.

Winter storms made way for the cold blast of spring, and finally the weather eased, bringing a flood of daffodils and crocuses to the borders.

Stephanie reflected, sometimes, that it was a good thing she hadn't believed all Rory's protestations of infatuation. More time had passed now, since that confused time with Rory, than had passed between her holiday romance with Tass and her ridiculous decision to seek him out. But no way was she going to seek out Rory. She'd learned her lesson, and wouldn't embarrass herself a second time.

But in the privacy of her own bedroom, sometimes she tapped Rory's name into the search engine to follow the breaking story of his marina development.

Once the finance had been sorted the proposals had gone to press, engendering a whole raft of hostile responses: lobbying from locals who alleged that the massive change would affect their lifestyles; lobbying from eco warriors about the damage to the surrounding salt marsh; and lobbying by an action group who felt that every individual in the community should be compensated financially for the disruption to their town.

She shook her head. Those who wanted a bite of the pie were as vociferous as those who wanted to see him fail, but no-one wanted to stand by Rory and help him achieve something that might ultimately benefit the town. She wondered whether the whole thing would simply fold under the pressure, whether Rory's finances would be eaten up before the development got anywhere near being started.

Poor Rory. All those dreams, and he'd simply put himself in the position of pariah within his own community.

There were many images of him on line: shaking hands with the financiers, arguing with lobbyists, discussing plans with wildlife experts, standing at the door of his old buildings, before his own ageing yacht, and next to an image of the fairly conservative buildings that had been planned.

She mentally envisaged him disappearing under a swathe of paperwork, and wondered whether he had managed to get himself a secretary with enough initiative to take a load from his shoulders, as she would have done.

Stephanie viewed all this deliberately from an emotional distance. She'd been hurt when he hadn't returned her calls, but somehow the fact that he hadn't called proved how unfounded her hopes had been. If he'd really wanted her, if there had been even the *possibility* of wanting her, he would have called.

Work, meanwhile, had become something that stimulated her interest rather than an eight-hour penance for her lack of drive when she had been eighteen. She no longer rose in the morning knowing she was about to count down another day, but often came to her job earlier than was required as there was something that needed her attention.

Management, she decided, wasn't rocket science. It didn't require an exceptional brain or in-depth financial perception, but rather, people skills and common sense, which she had in abundance.

She was in the downstairs office, situated at one end of the workroom, slogging her way through a pile of orders for fine silk lace, when Marie buzzed and asked her to go upstairs. She ran up, two at a time, and stopped short at Marie's office.

Rory, dressed in a smart suit, was sitting with her, his briefcase on his lap. It was the same old briefcase, she noted, with the hole in one corner as if it had been nibbled by mice.

He was different, though. Clean shaven, smart, and his hair, if not exactly styled, was certainly shorter. And there was a new set of lines around his mouth and eyes that hadn't been there before.

Marie was watching her reaction closely. 'Stephanie, Rory Banner, here, says he knows you. He'd like a word.'

There was a question behind the comment. If she said no, Rory would be shown the door, no matter who he was or what he wanted.

'Rory,' she said guardedly.

He rose to his feet, and if he'd had a hat it would have been mangled between his fingers, she felt sure. The expression on his face was that of a schoolboy who'd been sent to the headmaster.

'Stephanie, can we talk?'

'Ah, I'm not sure what we have to talk about.'

There was a brief silence as he assimilated that comment, then he shook his head. 'No. No, I can't accept that. I won't. We have a lot to talk about. If you're not ready, I can come back.'

'But – why now? After all this time?'

'I need to know why you ran away.'

Marie was glancing from one to the other, bemusement turning to amusement.

'How about you take an early lunch, Stephanie? Take all the time you need. Have a drink.'

'But –'

'Consider it an order.'

Rory's brow rose as he glanced back at Marie, and they shared a smile that seemed to exclude Stephanie.

She followed Rory down the stairs to the foyer.

'Where shall we go?' he asked.

'There's a pub just around the corner that does food, but I don't think –'

'Lead the way.'

'How did you find me here?'

'I found your mother. She told me. She was curious, to say the least. She had no idea who I was; you didn't mention me to her?'

'No. She would have done well as an inquisitor.'

'I believe she would.'

'Here,' she said, stopping by a small door with a dark stained-glass window declaring: Public bar.

Inside, he went to the bar. 'Beer or wine?'

'Water please.'

'Two pints and a menu, please,' he requested over the top of her protestations. She shrugged assent at the bar man.

'I can't do this without a drink, and I won't drink alone,' Rory said, leading the way to a cast iron table by a small, high window. It was a typical town pub, small and cosy, with minimal lighting.

She stared downward, guessing that if the lighting were to be raised she would see cigarette burns on the carpet, it was that old.

'I don't see why you've come here now. I'm over Tass, and I'm over you.'

'Thank you for being so hurtfully blunt.' He looked the menu over. 'You're right, this does look like good pub grub. I'll go for the steak and Guinness pie, with chips. What will you have?'

'I don't really want –'

He waved the bar man over. 'Two Steak and Guinness pie, with chips, please, and some real veg if you can stump it up.'

'No problem,' the barman said, but he didn't look happy.

He thinks we're having a marital spat, she thought.

'Believe it or not,' Rory said, 'this is as difficult for me as it is for you. I wavered about coming, and backed off more times than I can tell you. I wasn't that brave. But I couldn't just leave it. If you tell me to, I'll go away and you'll never see me again. But I couldn't just give you up without a fight.'

'But that's what you *did*,' she said, bemused.'

'Not willingly. I thought it was what you wanted, but I didn't know what loneliness meant until you burst into my life, then just upped and ran away.'

'I tried to call you,' she said in a low voice. 'I called your mobile, and I called your home, several times over the following weeks, but you never answered.'

Another long silence, then he sighed. 'Did you, really?'

'Why would I lie?'

'I went home and found the place tidy, and you packed up and gone. I was gobsmacked. I didn't think you would have done that, but you did.'

'I left you a note.'

'There was no note.'

'I don't see how you could have missed it. It was right on top of your filing, on the table. I told you Mum had broken her arm. That's why I had to rush off. I said I'd call when I knew what was happening. You know I did. *And* I left a message on your mobile.'

'I got that all right. You said you had to leave for personal reasons. I thought you meant me. The moment I got that I rushed up to the cottage, but I was too late, you'd gone. I phoned your mobile several times, but you didn't answer.'

'I was probably driving.' Oh, god, she thought, was this all a catalogue of mistakes? 'I thought you'd come and find me, but you never did.'

'Of course I came. I had some things to sort out first. The development had reached a critical point, but I drove up a couple of days later, looking for you. I found your flat, but the girl there told me you'd moved out. I asked her where, and she said you'd told her on no account to pass that information on. She said you never wanted to see me again.'

'Rachel said that? The bitch! And you believed her?'

'She was very believable. I got in the truck and drove home. On the way I had a tantrum and threw the bloody mobile out of the window. I suspect it was disassembled by the next passing truck. I had to buy a new one.'

She almost smiled.

'So that's why I couldn't get you on your mobile.'

'Of course, then, I couldn't remember your mobile number, and was never at the cottage. I couldn't bear to be there anymore. It was too empty.'

'Oh, Lord. I think I need a whiskey.'

'Me, too.'

For the first time, she lifted her eyes to meet his. 'Was it really real?'

'What I felt for you? What I still feel for you?'

'Oh, Lord.'

'Is it too late?'

At that moment the barman came over and fussed with condiments and cutlery. 'Your meals are about ready, sir, is there anything else?'

'A couple of whiskeys, please,' Sophie said. 'Big ones.'

'You haven't answered my question.'

'I, ah, don't quite know what you're asking.'

'Have you got another boyfriend?'

'No, but –'

'Then it's not too late,' he said with satisfaction. 'Here's dinner. Eat first, then we can make the arrangements for you to come and start working for me.' She froze. His brows raised. 'That was a joke.'

Back at the office, Marie took one look at them, and sighed. 'I suppose this means I'll have to get another Trainee Manager for the factory?'

'Absolutely,' Rory said.

'Will you stop acting as though you can make my decisions for me?' Stephanie said, exasperated.

Rory gave his slow smile. 'You have no idea how bossy I can be. Now, I'm going to let you get on with your work, and find a hotel for the night. You'll need to talk to your mother without me being there. Tomorrow I'm going to ask you to come home with me for the weekend, no strings attached. Think about it.'

Chapter 10

Huddled into the far corner of the noisy truck on Friday evening, Stephanie didn't have to find an excuse not to talk. She was happy to watch Rory's profile, albeit in stunned disbelief that she was really there.

He was concentrating on driving through a gradually darkening road, glancing at her now and again for some kind of reassurance. She had to admit he was one of the most stable and contented men she'd ever met.

Also, a determined one.

He'd insisted that she come back with him, in the truck, and he would bring her back to work Monday morning.

'Humour me,' he'd said. 'I was kind of rushing, before, but this time we're going to take it slowly, and do it right; and this time there's no baggage between us. I want you to come to me when you're good and ready.'

'You're so sure I will?'

'Nope. Just hopeful.'

Even though she had serious doubts about

their possible long-term prospects, he seemed to be absolutely confident, happy to believe in her. It was strange how comfortable that certainty made her feel – when she wasn't worrying.

No-one had ever wanted her badly enough to be as resolute as he was being now. It was quite flattering, sending a warm glow through her middle, but she didn't mistake it for love. She told herself she'd merely decided to go along with him to give herself time to prove him wrong.

In the back of her mind, though, a small, devil lurked, asking her whether she hadn't wished, just a tiny bit, to see what would have happened had she sent him packing. That thought continued to plague her all the way to the South Coast. Would he truly have simply driven away as he'd promised?

That she doubted it, had a good-feel factor.

When they arrived at the cottage the pink glow on the horizon had faded to black and the air was chill. Rory walked around the truck, opened her door and held his hand out hesitantly, his eyes meeting hers for the first time in two hours.

He wasn't confident at all, Stephanie realised as she put her own in it and jumped down. Rory squeezed her hand with intimate acknowledgment.

Then, lifting his weathered face to the faint breeze, he sniffed with satisfaction. 'It's good to be home.'

The warmth of his eyes and the strength in his arm reminded her he'd said it wasn't home without her. It was too lonely. As though she made his house a home. It *was* good to be back here, after thinking she'd left it behind forever, and to think of it as home was even better.

He led her in and switched on the lights.

It was as chilly inside as out.

'It'll warm up soon,' he said. 'The heating cut in half an hour ago, but I brought some wood in, just in case. I'll light a fire.'

Just in case his mission had been successful, and he brought her back? It was daft, but she imagined him coming here to the cold house, sitting on his own in the dark with the unlit fire a kind of penance.

But, no. If she hadn't come back with him, he'd have gone to the hut and wouldn't have come here at all. He said he'd mostly lived there since his mother left, and continued to do so once she disappeared out of his life. When the building works started, the hut would probably be demolished in the face of progress. Where would he live, then?

She sighed.

He looked up, a lit match in his hand.

'What?'

'It's all so complicated.'

He lit the fire. 'No, it's not. It's simple. I love you. I want you to live here with me. Other people are making it difficult, but we won't let them win.'

'Rory, if I'd never met Tass, would we have been together at all?'

'I think I would have eventually found the courage to look for you. But don't let him in, not tonight. I want you to think of times ahead, when we're married and our kids are running about the place.'

'Good Lord, you have it all sorted; *it was meant to be*, and all that kind of shite?'

He grinned. 'No. I don't believe in fate. That's why I had to come and get you. If I'd left it to fate you'd have eventually gone off with some other guy, and I'd have had to go to the trouble of chatting up some other woman to be my wife. Or maybe not.'

'You said there had been one, once. She let you down.'

'I told you that, did I? It was nothing. Just a foolish teenage thing. But I was hurt at the time.'

'And you've never had serious intentions towards any other woman in all that time?'

The fire burst into life. 'I wasn't celibate, and there were a few I tried to love, but no.

And if I'd had a hundred women in that time, would it matter to you as long as you were the one I loved, and the one I asked to marry me?'

'A hundred? Honestly? Yes.'

He chuckled.

'You see there are some things that don't need to be shared, we all have a past. But you can be sure of one thing: I never seduced anyone with false promises.'

'I thought we weren't inviting *him* in tonight.'

He sat back on his heels. 'I don't know what we can do to get rid of him, do you? Will he always be there, between us?'

She shuddered. 'I hope not.'

'But you love me.'

'I've never said as much.'

'I'd love it if you'd say it, but you've told me many times. Every gesture, every look, that kiss on the beach. You knew then. You just haven't learned to believe it, but you will.'

Stephanie folded her arms defensively.

Rory stood back. 'There. That's the fire going, now for the seductive candle-lit dinner.'

'I thought you didn't cook?'

'It's all pre-cooked, sterilised, hermetically sealed, and frozen. Except the wine, and that's just nicely chilled.'

A small flutter of amusement hovered on the corners of Stephanie's mouth.

'Just what is it you're going to poison me with?'

'Well, it calls itself lasagne on the packet.'

'I haven't eaten all day, we could give it a shot.'

'Good, I'll press the on-button on the food zapper. Would you like a glass of wine?'

'On an empty stomach?'

'Definitely.'

Stephanie chuckled.

He poured two glasses, put them on the coffee table, and plonked himself beside her on the sofa. 'Do you mind?'

'No.'

He shuffled closer. 'Do you mind that?'

'No.'

'That's better.'

He put his arm around her. 'Aren't you glad to be here?'

'I guess so.'

His face creased fractionally with pleasure, and the sight sent a shiver of desire through her. After six months, and the absolute conviction that this had all been a lie, she was almost disconcerted at the speed with which life had taken another about- turn.

Rory gave her a slight hug.

'I love just being with you,' he confessed,

his eyes caressing. 'But I want more.'

Stephanie smiled uncertainly.

'It's OK, no pressure.'

'A couple of days ago, I knew I wasn't ever going to see you again, so I'm finding this a bit – strange.'

He bent his head and kissed her. Words fled. They were kissing, not with uncontrollable passion, but as if some deep inner decision had been made, regardless of circumstances.

Whatever doubts Stephanie had experienced when she was alone were washed away on the tide of the desire which flooded her when she was with him.

It was no lie. She loved him.

'You're so lovely I could eat you,' Rory said eventually, 'but dinner awaits. I'll bring it in by the fire.'

'Well, was it OK?' Rory asked, finally.

'I hate to think what was in it, but it tasted fine.'

'More wine?'

'Are you trying to get me drunk?'

'No, just accommodating.'

He poured more dry wine into the tall glasses.

She swilled hers around, catching the flames inside the glass. 'I'm cooked on one side, cold on the other,' she admitted.

'Yes, if this is going to be our home, we need to get some double glazing and insulation sorted out, and I'll fix that door. I've been meaning to for years. I just didn't have the incentive.'

The tiles around the fire glowed brightly and the velvet curtain wafted gently from the door as the wind from the sea bumped fitfully against the cottage. The window panes rattled, and every so often a cloud of smoke belched back into the room; but somehow all that going on outside made the cottage a haven, a secure nest from which they didn't want to escape.

They talked away the evening, Stephanie told Rory about Rachel stealing her job, and how she'd put Rachel's application in the bin.

'I felt really bad about that, afterwards.'

'She deserved it.'

'Yes, but I was taking advantage of my situation.'

'It's only human, and you wouldn't have wanted her working in the same place as you.'

'No, she'd have poisoned Marie against me. Or she would have tried, anyway.'

'Not a good scenario. But Marie looked like the sort of person who would make her own mind up. So, you're going to hand your notice in on Monday.'

'Maybe.'

'Maybe, why?'

'Because.'

'Because why?'

'You said you weren't going to push me. I just have to take my time. And I'm not going to run out on Marie. She believed in me, and she's the only one who ever did.'

'Except me.'

'That's different.'

'I hope so.'

'Now, I want to know about you. What was it like, growing up, here?'

Rory told her about his rough and ready upbringing, working with his father during the lean times when he should have been at school. That he had loved his father, and now missed him was evident. Everything he said filled her with a sense of belonging, a sense of rightness of things as they were.

Eventually the fire finally died to a pile of glowing embers. She leaned back against Rory's chest, and his chin dropped to brush against her hair, his arms wrapping around her possessively. Her hand rested lightly on his thigh. It was so safe, so comfortable she didn't want to move.

Then he broke the spell.

One moment his breath was a subtle, erotic

torment against her neck, then he kissed it gently, and whispered softly, 'I want to make love to you, sweet Stephanie.'

She tensed spontaneously as he echoed the words Tass had once used.

Rory sighed, misunderstanding. 'You're not ready. No matter, I can wait.'

He didn't ask again, but just held her closely without talking, almost an apology for mentioning it, but the magic was gone.

Later, huddled on her own between the cold covers, Stephanie wondered again what it was that made her keep pushing Rory away, when she wanted, as much as he did, to remove the final barriers.

But really, she knew.

Rory had persuaded her to come and stay at his house, but he would never persuade her to make love to him, which he could easily do, the way she felt about him. She had allowed herself to be seduced once, and the consequences still disturbed her. When she made love to Rory it would be the beginning of a lifetime's commitment, or she would not make love to him at all. Her time with Tass made her feel cheap, in hindsight. She was afraid it would drive a wedge through any chance of happiness she might discover with Rory, but Tass, would never have taken no for an answer, and she'd been so needy. If she had continued to resist, he would have simply dumped her, and looked for someone else. Maybe she'd instinctively known that, even back then. Their loving had been as consuming as the fire, which now emitted a final lazy curl of smoke before giving up the ghost.

She was thinking of him again.

Tass was still a dark shadow between her and Rory. He held onto her even now, as selfish in death as he had been in life. She didn't see how she would ever be rid of that guilt she carried because of him, and could never openly admit her love to Rory until Tass was gone, but she couldn't see a way of ridding her mind of his presence. Rory said her relationship with Tass worried her more than it worried him; he was right. It bothered her mightily.

But what bothered her more was the certainty that Rory was hiding something about how he died. That wasn't a good place to start a lasting relationship.

Chapter 11

Stephanie was woken out of sleep the next morning by the insistent ringing of a telephone. It didn't give up, and Rory didn't wake, so eventually she climbed out of bed and scrambled down the cold stairs wrapped in her coat.

'Hello?'

'Oh, it's you.'

Jimmy's voice was blunt to the point of rudeness. Stephanie had forgotten about the antipathy of the native Townsea population, a nail in the coffin of her happiness.

'Yes, it's me,' she said shortly.

There was a pregnant silence, then Jimmy said unexpectedly. 'I'm sorry, you just took me by surprise. I didn't think...'

'It doesn't matter. Do you want Rory?'

'I don't need to speak to him. Tell him that if he wants to see father, he'd better come on down this morning.'

'Your father? I don't understand.'

'He's dying.'

'Oh. I'm sorry.'

She flushed, though he couldn't see it. She didn't know the man, but what else could you say?

'Yes, well. I've got some other calls to make. See you around.'

Stephanie went and woke Rory.

He rose out of sleep like a grumpy bear, all stubble and annoyance, then, realising who had woken him, he reached up and tumbled her onto the bed beside him, rolling over and squashing her under his bulk.

'Morning, gorgeous,' he said, nuzzling at the opening of her coat with his lips.

'Not now,' Stephanie said pushing ineffectually at his shoulders, enjoying the rasp of his unshaven chin against her skin. The seriousness of her expression made him release her. 'Jimmy just phoned. He said you should go and see his father.'

'Oh.' He raked his hand through his hair, understanding instantly. 'Go and get dressed. I'll only be a moment.'

'They won't want me there.'

'I do. They can get used to the idea.' He smiled fractionally. 'Besides. I don't want to come back and find you gone, it would be such a hassle to have to go to the trouble of chasing you down again.'

She glowed at the thought but said

logically, 'How would I go? There's not a wealth of public transport down here.'

'Oh, no. Forgot.'

'I could hitch.'

'Do that, and I *will* tan your hide.'

He climbed out of bed, and Stephanie fled; but not before she'd glimpsed the way his body sloped to tight creamy buttocks, untouched by the sun.

Martin Purdie's cottage was off a little grass-rutted lane outside Townsea on the same side as the church. The low-ceilinged row of cottages was picturesque, the situation quaint. They looked out to the sea over the tops of the shops and the hotels which had sprung up during the last century. Stephanie could see that they'd fetch good prices today, for the location alone.

The front door was open, and looked as if it had remained that way through most of its life. Jimmy met them with no more than a fleeting lift of the brows at Stephanie's presence, and let them to a downstairs bedroom that had probably once been a dining room.

Martin Purdie's breath was erratic, he was struggling to breathe. He was emaciated, his skin translucent with impending death. His brother, Thomas, sat beside him, holding his hand, for all the world like a garden gnome, just waiting.

Rory went forward and spoke to the men, but now Stephanie held back. She shouldn't be here, she knew. It wasn't her place.

Jimmy, taking pity, drew her back out into the kitchen. 'There's tea on the hob,' he said. 'Help yourself.'

He turned to walk away, but Stephanie blurted out, 'I didn't want to come. I didn't want to intrude, but Rory didn't want to leave me alone.'

He pursed his lips, his green eyes assessing, then he smiled. It was an open smile which flooded his whole face somehow, distancing him from memories of Tass. 'Rory loves you, doesn't he?'

'He says he does, but it's difficult –' she bit the words off. Jimmy was the wrong person to be talking to, especially at this time, but it was out before she realised.

'He understands about Tass.'

She nodded, thankfully. 'But it's too soon, hard to believe it's not just another mistake.'

'Don't muddle Rory with Tass,' Jimmy said. 'Rory's worth a hundred of him, and don't you forget it.'

Unexpectedly, he came and sat opposite her at the small table, and held his hand out.

'Look, I'm sorry I was rude to you before.

We had a few issues. Am I forgiven?'

Stephanie reached for it instinctively. 'I thought you all hated me,' she said candidly.

'It wasn't personal. We had a lot to cope with.'

'And me coming back rubbed salt in the wound, I guess. I'm sorry. It was unintentional.'

'Did you really love Tass?'

There was serious question in the level gaze.

'No. No I don't think so, though, at the time I wouldn't have said that.'

'Then why all the questions?'

'I just wanted to know the truth.' Colour burned through her face, and she looked away. 'I can't be fair to Rory while Tass hangs like a shadow between us.'

Memories of gut-wrenching obsession came briefly to mind, and she buried them. 'It was like tasting the forbidden fruit. He left a sour taste in my mouth. I'm trying to wash it away, but it doesn't want to go.' She glanced up guiltily. 'Tass was your cousin, I shouldn't be talking to you like this.'

'I understand. It's all right. Sometimes there's a very thin line between love and hate. I still don't know if I discovered it.'

She guessed he was talking about his own relationship with Tass. 'I cried when I learned he'd died,' she said. 'Not because I had any real hopes of a future with him, but because he had been so vibrant, so vital. It seemed so wicked that someone so *alive* could just cease to exist.'

She glanced at him for understanding.

'I cried at his funeral, too,' Jimmy admitted. 'In spite of everything.'

He might have said more, but there was a querulous cry from the adjoining room. 'Jimmy? Jimmy?'

Jimmy scraped his chair back and ran. Stephanie followed, but waited in the shadow of the door.

'I'm here, Dad.'

The old man had been struggling fretfully against the covers. 'Don't go diving, son, promise me.'

'I won't,' he said softly.

'I'm afraid...'

'There's nothing to be afraid of anymore, Dad.'

'Oh. Yes. Tass is dead, God forgive him.'

Stephanie looked beyond the room, out of a tiny window, at the great arc where the sea met the sky. She hadn't been meant to hear that. Nothing to be afraid of anymore. Now that Tass is dead. The words burned into her brain like brands. She could see them glowing behind her eyelids as she closed her eyes fractionally with the horror of understanding.

She looked at the old man. She'd never seen him in life, but in impending death his face was stark and strong-boned, reminiscent of Tass. They were very similar in build, these Purdies.

You couldn't tell a person's character from looks alone, though. Thomas, Martin, and Jimmy were of one stock, Tass and his runaway father from some other strain. Who knew what had made them different.

Jimmy was holding his father's hand now, and Rory had his arm around the girl, Janet, who was hugging a baby to her breast.

The old man seemed to sink into the bed. His eyelids fluttered and closed. He didn't see the tears which trickled almost unnoticed down Thomas's lined cheeks.

Tass is dead, God forgive him Thomas had said to her all those months ago, and at the time the significance had not penetrated her understanding, but it now hit her with the full force as she realised the burden he was carrying.

And now, she recalled, Rory had said it was Tass's greed that had killed him. It hadn't registered at the time, but the burden they were all carrying now hit her with full force. With a certainty that brought bile to her mouth, Stephanie discerned the secret that Jimmy and Rory had been keeping from her.

At what point Martin Purdie died, Stephanie wasn't sure. Realisation only dawned as she saw grief materialise on Jimmy's face now that deception wasn't necessary. It occurred to her that Jimmy now owned the cottage, and could sell up and leave if he wished, but somehow, she knew he'd stay. He belonged here.

If it had been Jimmy who had died beneath the girder in the old wreck, Tass would have inherited this cottage, now. He probably would have sold up and gone before the old man's body was cold in the grave. He would have found it hard to conceal the unholy joy that would have arisen at Martin's death.

She stumbled unnoticed out of the door and made her way through the silent streets down to the sea-front. Her stomach heaved with the horror of her knowledge, but she stilled the nausea, and walked on. They had clanned together to keep the true nature of Tass's character from her and everyone else, and Jimmy had taken the fall. They were keeping the family integrity intact; but it wasn't Jimmy they were shielding.

It was Tass.

Horror flooded as she pictured Tass below the water sawing off the bolts and making the girder deliberately unsafe; a trap for his own cousin. Had Tass really been that callous? Could he have given the bolt a final tug as Jimmy swam below? And if the girder hadn't done the job, would he have wrenched the gag from Jimmy's mouth to finish it? Could he have stood by and watched understanding and despair fill Jimmy's eyes as he drowned? Just so that he could inherit Martin's cottage. That he'd been caught in his own trap had been poetic justice. But his family would say nothing, so that those who loved him could mourn his passing.

Stephanie blundered along the seafront dazed by this revelation. Jimmy's silence had been for the sake of his family. He'd allowed the papers to crucify him so that the truth would never be aired in public.

Tass had planned a murder, not Jimmy.

He might have succeeded had the sea not played its joker. He should have listened to the old fisherman at the quay. *He should have had more care to the sea, she was ever a cruel mistress.* But truly, Tass had been betrayed, not by his mistress, the sea, but by his own cold-hearted ambitions.

A chill breeze hit Stephanie's face, but she carried on blindly towards the cliff, and struggled up the slick path to the old look-out station, and from there stared darkly out across the bay.

The family's grief brought a lump to her throat.

What they had lived with these last months! Not the knowledge of a loved boy's death, but the knowledge that he had died rigging a trap designed to murder his own cousin.

'Damn you, Tass Purdie,' she said softly, while rain seeped like tears from the sky.

Last time she'd been up here the storm had echoed her grief, and she had nearly fallen to her death through love of a green-eyed seducer. This time, the pitiful thin drizzle, whipped into needles by an offshore wind, echoed the pity she felt for him.

He had never been satisfied with what he had, and never would have been. Nothing would ever have been enough, she realised. No matter what he took out of life, he would have always wanted what remained just out of reach. What other ruined lives would have been strewn in his search for the unobtainable?

'It's as well you died, Tass,' she whispered.

No answer came back to haunt her from the depths of the cold, grey sea. No wind called her name with the seductive green-eyed promise of a forbidden future. It had all been a macabre joke, a tragedy in the true sense of the word.

'Stephanie!'

The voice was no echo from a dark dream, but a worried, concerned cry. She turned and watched Rory run frantically up the cliff-path towards her, his muscles bunching with effort, his mouth gasping for breath. Stephanie had never seen such a wonderful sight. She loved him with all her heart. He slowed down as he saw the look on her face, not knowing whether to reach for her or not, afraid that she laboured under some vast grief.

'I know what happened,' she told him.

'No one really knows. Are you all right?'

She nodded. 'He's gone, Rory. I came up here to tell him it was over, but he's gone already.'

She held out her arms, and Rory hugged her close, sighing with relief. 'He could never take rejection,' he said. 'He didn't stay to hear it from you.'

'And Martin?'

'He's gone. Thomas and Jimmy will see to the details.' He hesitated, then added. 'You might as well know the rest. Janet was Jimmy's girlfriend, and Tass stole her because he could, then dumped her the day you showed up.'

She winced. 'Oh. Poor girl.'

'Yes. Jimmy has forgiven her, but she still hasn't managed to forgive herself. Maybe she never will. You see, it's Tass's child.'

'What will she do?'

'Jimmy's going to marry her. He'll take on Tass's child as if it were his own. They called her Mary, after Jimmy's mother. I'm trusting you with this, you understand.'

'Thank you.'

Stephanie shuddered faintly, hoping that whatever bad thread had slipped into the weaving of Tass's character was not growing within his child.

Rory took her hand to lead her safely down the cliff path.

'Rory?'

'Yes?'

'I do love you. I've known it for a while.'

'Of course you have, my sweet Stephanie.'

'Do you still want to marry me?'

'I thought you'd never ask.'

He drove her up to the cottage, leaving the spectre of Tass behind, lonely on the water.

If you enjoyed this romance, be proactive: write a review on Amazon. Your views matter

To Claim your FREE ebook
Once Bitten Twice Shy
visit my website: www.chrislewando.com

If you would like any other novels in Large Print Paperback, please let me know via my website.

check out my other novels...

Buried Desire

Althea Caradoc is an archaeologist, passionate about the past, embarking on an excavation before the proposed new Motorway obliterates the evidence.

Jack Chadwyck is the landowner fighting for his present. He resents the proposed Motorway that is going to tear his land in two and resents the archaeologists from disturbing his last year of peace.

When Althea calls him a barbarian, it tempts him to act like one. With respect to the bewitching girl, who is surely too young to be managing the project, he is both entranced and aggravated.

In order to save himself he must overcome his own prejudices, and somehow win her trust.

A gentle romance with strong, modern characters who battle with their own flaws in order to reap the rewards they both seek.

Breaking Trust

Rose Trethwick, an artist, born and bred in America, comes to England to claim a small cottage left to her by her paternal grandmother. But in order to inherit, she must live in the house for three months. She falls in love with it, knowing that was what her estranged grandmother was hoping.

William Montacue, the owner of the estate, turns out to be the most attractive and attentive man Rose has ever met. But the estate is in financial difficulties, and he needs the cottage to fulfil his own dreams.

Rose wonders how far he's prepared to go to make his own plans come true. Is he in love with her or her inheritance? All of which is complicated by the machinations of William's brother and uncle who both stand to gain if the long-standing entail binding the estate is broken.

Each has a different story to tell – but who is lying, and what is the secret that caused Rose's father to run away to America to seek his fortune?

Lonely at Pinehaven

When Sarah's parents are killed in a motor accident, and she inherits her father's business, everything changes. She realises that Robert, her long-standing fiancé, wants the business more than he wants her, so breaks up with him, and finds herself alone.

All Sarah's friends have known her and Robert as a couple for a long time, so when her doctor tells her to take a break before she has a massive breakdown, she chooses to take an extended stay at a private hotel her parents used to patronise.

There, she meets Ashley, the owner's son, whose marriage had dramatically failed a few years previously, leaving him mistrustful of women in general. Complications arise when Ashley's wife dumps their six-year old child at the hotel. The traumatised six-year-old desperately needs to learn the meaning of trust, and provides a conduit through which Ashley and Sarah might heal their respective wounds – if they can individually let go of past mistakes.

Once Bitten, Twice Shy

Fiona was dumped by her boyfriend, and is miserably wallowing in self-pity, when her friend Suzie begs her to take a temporary secretarial post with Adam, the advertising mogul. He's a testosterone-filled, conceited, egotistical, larger-than-life bully, she says, who is never seen without a six-foot, blue-eyed blonde hanging off him like an ornament. Fiona doubts he'll even notice her. After all, she's short, with brown hair and eyes the colour of bog water.

Adam is intrigued. He's never had a secretary who didn't look like Barbie, and he's not used to being argued with. Their relationship is a meeting of opposing forces. Within an hour Fiona is fired and hired again... what is it about her, that he can't just let her go?

And can she allow herself to believe that this amazingly successful and talented man, with a history of high-flying conquests, has truly fallen in love with her? After all, he creates TV advertising. He's a master of deception, and can sell anything to anybody...

Published by Drombeg Press in 2018

Chrislewando.com

47947984R00143

Printed in Poland
by Amazon Fulfillment
Poland Sp. z o.o., Wrocław